THE NAME OF THE WORLD

DENIS JOHNSON

THE NAME OF THE WORLD

Perennial

An Imprint of HarperCollinsPublishers

First Perennial edition published 2001.

Designed by Christine Weathersbee

The Library of Congress has catalogued the hardcover edition as follows:

Johnson, Denis.
    The name of the world / Denis Johnson.—1st ed.
      p. cm.
    ISBN 0-06-019248-8
    1. College teachers—Middle West—Fiction. 2. Loss
(Psychology)—Fiction. 3. Middle West—Fiction. 4. Widowers—
Fiction. I. Title.
    PS3560.O3745 N36 2000
    813'.54—dc21   99-085970

ISBN 0-06-092965-0 (pbk.)

01 02 03 04 05 ❖/RRD 10 9 8 7 6 5 4 3 2 1

For Cha and Ellie

THE NAME OF THE WORLD

Since my early teens I've associated everything to do with college, the "academic life," with certain images borne toward me, I suppose, from the TV screen, in particular from the films of the 1930s they used to broadcast relentlessly when I was a boy, and especially from a single scene: Fresh-faced young people come in from an autumn night to stand around the fireplace in the home of a beloved professor. I smell the bonfire smoke in their clothes and the professor's aromatic pipe tobacco, and I feel the general, unquestioned sweetness of youth, of autumn, of college—the sweetness of this life. Not that I was ever in love with this dream, or even particularly drawn to it. It's just that I concluded it existed somewhere. My own undergraduate career stretched over six or seven years, interrupted by bouts of work and transfers to a second and then a third institution, and I remember it all as a succession of requirements and endorsements. I didn't attend the football games. I don't remember coming across any bonfires. By several of my teachers I was impressed, even awed, and their influence shaped me as much as anything else along the way, but I never had a look inside any of their homes. All this by way of saying it came as a surprise, the gratitude with which I accepted an invitation to teach at a university.

When the chance came along, I was nearly fifty. After college I'd taught high school for better than a decade, earning postgraduate credits in the summers. One day I wrote a letter to a presidential candidate, advising him on policy and strategy (this was Senator Thomas Thom of Oklahoma; he faded early in the primaries), and although I'd had no idea people who wrote such letters were ever heeded, much less hired, in a blink I went from Mr. Reed the Social Studies person to Mike Reed the speechwriter, staff floater, and cloakroom confidant, and spent nearly twelve years in Washington. I quit just after Senator Thom began his fifth term. I took the job at the University when my book idea was turned down—I'd offered to witness to power's corrupting influence, but apparently no such witness was required.

Then I found myself in the Comparative Studies wing of the Humanities Building, although I was actually an Adjunct Associate Professor of History. (The Humanities Department was long ago dissolved to form more departments, bigger departments; the old building houses budgetary mavericks, grant-sponsored programs and the like, experiments that live out their funding periods and fade away. Somehow this became the home of History.) I ran small seminars, asking bright, undirected students to read books I'd already read and then listening while they presented papers to the rest of the group for criticism. In other words, I didn't do anything. This would have interfered not at all with a glorious future in that place, but I didn't bother with the other side of business there, either, the meetings and the memos and so on.

Four renewals was about the limit for my type of appointment, and I was near the end of my third. After next year, they'd move me along. Meanwhile, I was on vacation.

But people in positions like mine have to keep alert for new ones, and so I found myself one evening dining in a group of eleven at the home of Ted MacKey, Chairman of the School of Music. The surroundings came close to the 1930s moving picture of this life: the snowflakes coming down outside in a college-town night that threatened to add to itself the jingling of sleigh bells and the songs of young carolers, while inside the house, lodge-like in its dimensions, we all drank hot buttered rum around a warm blaze that sent a changing light under the lustrous mantel and onto windows of leaded glass, and onto a black antique telescope and a monstrous beige globe I would have bet presented the world as it had been long ago, but would never be again. We drank hot buttered rum in the atmosphere, in other words, of a very expensive gift shop. It oppressed me. It oppressed me although I'd been given my supper in plenty of homes exactly like it at other universities and in Washington, and I'd even eaten here at Ted MacKey's, two winters previous. It oppressed me for that thought as much as any other, maybe, the mental image of a thousand such dwellings pressed window to window across the wide undifferentiated air of a plunging chasm, and me with a spoon and a bowl and a smile in every one of them.

The dinner that night honored a distinguished visitor to our campus, the Israeli composer Izaak Andropov. As it happened, he'd taken a fever, and didn't attend.

I was here to make a new acquaintance, the head of a University fiefdom called the Forum for Interpretive Scholarship. The Forum had money. They had Associate-level jobs. They had offices, salaries, everything. Best of all they had no duties, no classes. Or so Ted MacKey had promised me, letting out this information in a casual way, as if I might not be looking around for another slot someplace the year after next. This happened all the time, that is, people I hardly knew often suggested, one way or another, that they'd like to help me. I was the object of much goodwill, in fact, sometimes because the man I'd worked for in Washington was disliked, and I'd quit him; or, conversely, because he was liked, and I'd worked for him. In any case, here was a chance to stretch out my vacation another academic year or two. Nothing ever happened at the Forum beyond an occasional presentation by one of the scholars, most of them emeriti from Big Ten universities and such, who just dragged out the lectures they'd been dragging out this way since the days when Ted MacKey's big beige globe had known what it was talking about.

I don't think any of the guests knew each other more than casually, but we didn't have to struggle much for things to say, as Ted MacKey had arranged a short concert for us. A young woman played the guitar and another the cello, after which Ted's grade-school son played the lute with astonishing self-possession, wearing pajamas and a robe and fuzzy slippers, and concentrating, plainly, not on his fingers but on the truth of his music.

I was seated next to Dr. J. J. Stein, the one who pulled the strings at the Forum for Interpretive Scholarship. Some kind of Scotch broth was dealt out. Even if I was aware I'd enjoyed too many of them, I didn't mind these dinners, particularly at the University. I like being around people who like being where they are. In the scholarly world, the world of the mind, much more than in the world of politics, it's common to meet people who've truly earned their comfort, at least in a sense, having labored through and left behind the parts of childhood so unpleasant for scholars, brains, intellectuals. And here they are, respected and safe at last, while the others slug it out in the marketplace. Dr. J. J. Stein was the person I might have imagined if I'd been trying to visualize this meeting in advance, a happy, bearded, balding scholar. And he went on to make an explanation for me of a kind I might have expected, too—incredibly earnest thinkers always have to explain the names they choose for their projects, because the names mean absolutely nothing when you hear them—as to why "Forum" was just the right word, why only "Interpretive" conveyed the right sense, why, when you'd finished considering all the words in the English language, "Scholarship" had to be the one.

I wasn't sure how deliberate a job of selling had been set for me in Dr. J.J.'s mind, but it happened I had an idea I wanted to elaborate, one requiring research assistants and more than one office, the kind of enterprise that might rope in all sorts of scholars and result in an anthology of essays all on a theme, and this vision I produced for him while he interrupted with enthusiastic questions, and the cellist, just on the other side of him, got attractively tipsy. In the midst of this it occurred to me aloud that Dr. J.J. might write my anthology's introduction and make it an occasion for talking about his Forum. The cellist, one of Ted's grad students, developed a kind of ironic interest in the plan, and asked questions herself, and pretty soon started interrupting the Doctor's interruptions, chiefly by saying, almost exclusively by saying, "Oh—*really?*" A striking redhead in a dress of blue velvet, she sat at the head of the table: Halfway through the meal she'd moved around to Izaak Andropov's unclaimed place of honor. Her ivory cheeks and her ivory shoulders grew flushed, and her voice took on a musical and dangerous timbre. I'm not sure why it is that the experience of witnessing a talented young person make a slight fool of herself, at a stiff little gathering like this, is so pleasant. But as she began to draw the focus to our corner of the table, even to become memorable, I sensed my own spiel would be forgotten, and I wasn't entirely sorry for the fact.

After dessert, Ted took three or four of us up to a parapet above the house. From the third floor a corkscrew staircase entered a dome on the roof, a curious structure like a glassed-in birdcage, about eight feet in diameter, say, and without illumination, so that the little group of us stood suddenly in the night, and in the sky. The weather had cleared, the snow had blown off the glass, and there were stars and moonlit, decorative clouds in the black heavens. "This used to be a sort of widow's walk," Ted explained, "but you can see it's been turned into—well, I don't know what it was turned into, to tell you the truth. I bring people up here because I'm curious whether it's something with a recognizable purpose." None of us recognized its purpose. In the end, I was left up there to ponder it all with a woman named Heidi Franklin, a historian from the Art Department. A friendly but awkward woman, precise and despairing—a homely woman, and I think I have the license to make such a remark, because I'm homely, too, and older than she, so I was homely first. I'm cherubic, baby faced, past fifty but taken for years younger, with cheery blue eyes, and for all of that, homely. In the glittering dark we stood talking very softly, probably about the stars. Heidi may have been interested in a nightcap somewhere downtown; I might have been, too. That neither of us put our finger to the balance, so to speak, and urged it in that direction owed to a sense we probably shared, and I certainly felt, that we'd been left up here alone together by design. If I'd asked, I might have learned that she was single, as I was, or worse, maybe recently divorced, as I was recently widowed.

When I say recently, I don't mean it in the sense that I might have bought a car recently, or seen a movie recently. I'm speaking as I'd speak about the recent change in the earth's climate, or the recent war, the recent—I think that's clear enough. It had been nearly four years, long enough to make me eligible again. Other people seemed to think so, anyway, and I wasn't going to argue about it.

When it was somehow decided the evening was done, all the guests left together, and the drivers started up their cars and sat inside them with the doors open while everybody said goodbye a second time. Here and there among the evergreens, lumps of snow dropped from branch to branch and down to the ground, yanking at the boughs. We'd all covered ourselves in caps and scarves, all but the lady cellist, who went hatless and carried her coat over her shoulder. In the fluorescent light of the curbside arc lamps she looked ghastly, her blue velvet dress a sudden mournful black. I heard her say three words: "Sane? Or tame?" Her abundant red hair looked purple, her big blue eyes looked fake, inhuman, her lips stood out starkly in her face. She was talking to her date, she didn't know the rest of us existed, the aging rest of us, the sane, or tame, rest of us. I felt very kindly toward her, glad of her presence, maybe because she was drunk and didn't care about herself.

"I'm sorry we got sidetracked earlier," J. J. Stein told me as we parted. "Come around sometime. Just drop in. I'll show you around the Forum."

"Terrific. I look forward to it."

Ted MacKey, a tall, elegantly graying man, stood in the

amber warmth behind his windowglass, both hands uplifted in farewell. Ted wasn't quite as he first appeared. Over the rest of the winter he included me in a couple of other gatherings at his home, much less formal ones, and it turned out that he was a hipster, a gifted trumpeter who enjoyed a connection with all sorts of suave, tight-lipped, soft-spoken jazz musicians from up and down the Mississippi who ate his food, drank his booze, and improvised with him in trios and quartets. Not condescending to him in the least, I might add, but plainly honored to be playing with him, these men, sometimes women, who sent out their souls through their instruments, and otherwise expressed themselves, I noticed, only by tipping their heads, shrugging their shoulders, or slightly lowering their eyelids.

This was also Ted MacKey's style. Out of context it had seemed professorial. And just as people tended to get him wrong, he and our colleagues tended to get me wrong. I'd come among them as a man in shock, sickened by politics and at that time freshly, as opposed to recently, widowed. In the four years of our very slight acquaintance Ted had reinterpreted my ongoing paralysis as detachment, maybe irony. I was hip, I was beat. I could have sat in with Chet Baker, if I'd known how to play an instrument. As for my fellow teachers of history, they mistook my numbness for terror. They looked at me and saw somebody like J. Alfred Prufrock—looked at me and saw somebody like themselves.

The gatherings at Ted's were something of a relief. And not just from the meetings and occasional grim dinners with the stick figures we in the Department of History had made ourselves into, but also from the bleakness of my fourth winter here. The monthlong Christmas break was hard on the Department. I stayed in the empty college town, as I'd done every Christmas, and when classes resumed it seemed the other teachers had each, over the holidays, taken on some fearful form of suffering. Clara Frenow, the Chairperson, had been diagnosed with cancer and begun chemotherapy. Meanwhile our only colleague of color and the only one of us with something like a personality, a man named Tiberius Soames, an almost pathologically brilliant West Indian who conducted his large undergraduate lectures with such flourish he'd doubled the number of History majors since his advent here, tumbled suddenly into a psychic abyss and was hospitalized with severe depression. Two weeks after the winter break he was back, fragile and foreign, perpetrating a painful imitation of himself. Others fell under their own bad luck: a son arrested for drugs, a summer home burned to the ground with heirlooms inside, a case of writer's block and a textbook contract dissolved, and trouble between the young married couple who shared a full-time position.

Myself, I continued as I had for years. I showed up where I was invited. I read a great deal in the library. I went to the movies by myself. I watched the skaters on the campus pond. Quite a bit more than I'd have liked it known, I held imaginary conversations with a man named Bill, in which I went over the same ground I'd been going over since the deaths of my wife and daughter. While I went around looking paralyzed or detached, my thoughts ripped perpetually around a track like dogs after a mechanized rabbit.

Maybe this is why the young skaters looked so comfortable, even on the coldest days. In the daylight hours on what was called the Middle Campus, between the School of Law and the School of Social Sciences, from a dozen to as many as a hundred boys and girls glided around a pond with a tiny unscalable island in its center, a monolithic, rock island with a sculpture on its peak—red sheet-metal shapes—the pond marked off by a railing. Everybody skated around it in one direction. "Pond" may not be the right word. People told me it wasn't eight inches deep. A reflecting pool, I'd guess; about twice the area of a football field. There were always a few wobbly beginners clinging to the rail, but for the most part these young students sat on the pond's stone lip while they got on their skates, then stood up to take one long, expert stride onto an invisible carousel. It didn't look like exercise. No rabbit eluded them. They went in an endless loop, but they weren't after anything.

I often ate lunch in a cafeteria in the basement of the School of Law and then walked beside a bike path around the Middle Campus, stopping to watch the skaters until the chill forced me to start walking again, down past the pond and the Science Quad and over to the Museum of Art. And that's what I happened to do on February 20, the fourth anniversary of the accident that took my family. I watched the skaters, and then went to see Bill, the man with whom I was so sociable, as I've mentioned, in fantasy.

The friendship was all in my mind, but Bill was not. I saw him once or twice a week. He worked in the Museum of Art. I often visited a particular drawing there, and Bill was the guard who generally stood near it, wearing blue pants and a white shirt with a breast tag bearing his name: W. Connors. I introduced myself once, and he told me his first name. A black man, somewhere in his late forties.

That I should be so affected by this drawing as to come around all the time, hungering at it, I thought might be understandable to a person who'd spent enough time in its presence to have been penetrated, similarly penetrated, maybe without the complicity of the artgoer, but penetrated anyway by its message. I felt a kinship with Bill—an illusory kinship, like the strange shocking wedding you experience with a figure who turns his face toward you as you flicker past in a train—to inhabit a frame for them, as they inhabit a frame for you—looking from either side of the same frame, I think you get it, in a moment that blinks on and blinks off, but never changes, a picture, in other words. Anyhow I liked thinking we shared something, each of us involved so much with what was going on in the same frame, Bill Connors and I.

This picture was an anonymous work that almost anybody on earth could have made, but as it happened, a Georgia slave had produced it. The work's owners, the Stone family of Camden County, had found the work in the attic of the family's old mansion. It was drawn with ink on a large white linen bedsheet and consisted of a tiny single perfect square at the center of the canvas, surrounded by concentric freehand outlines. A draftsman using the right tools would have made thousands of concentric squares with the outlines just four or five millimeters apart. But, as I've said, the drawing, except for the central square, had been accomplished freehand: Each unintended imperfection in an outline had been scrupulously reproduced in the next, and since each square was larger, each imperfection grew larger too, until at the outermost edges the shapes were no longer squares, but vast chaotic wanderings.

To my way of thinking, this secret project of the nameless slave, whether man or woman we'll never know, implicated all of us. There it was, all mapped out: the way of our greatness. Though simple and obvious as an act of art, the drawing portrayed the silly, helpless tendency of fundamental things to get way off course and turn into nonsense, illustrated the church's grotesque pearling around its traditional heart, explained the pernicious extrapolating rules and observances of governments—implicated all of us in a gradual apostasy from every perfect thing we find or make.

Implicated. This wasn't my reaction only. I talked with lots of people who'd seen this work, and they all felt the same, but in various ways, if that makes sense. They felt uneasy around it, challenged, disturbed. I suppose that's what made it art, rather than drawing.

The piece wasn't beautiful, particularly, unless you like looking at tree rings on a fresh stump, and not as engrossing or as mystifying, in fact, as a piece of wood. Natural entities, the clouds, the sea, these are four-dimensional, and so is the slab of wood, because it invites you to consider that each ring took a year to make. The anonymous drawing was just a lot of sorrowful concentricity, but it spoke a truth. It made me in all matters a fundamentalist. I didn't go to "take it in." I went to be convicted.

I can't say I remember much about this particular visit to the museum. But I must have been troubled more than usual on this day, a bad anniversary, because I made the rest of it memorable by deciding to look up Heidi Franklin, the art historian with whom I'd hovered briefly in a capsule above the first few moments of this long winter, at Ted MacKey's house, in the widow's walk.

Whatever else I did in the museum that day, I must have had a wordless exchange with Bill in which we acknowledged one another perfunctorily and I wondered if he recognized me. Over these last four years he'd grown a mustache and acquired a chair in which he sat, these days, looking bored but not inattentive. Certainly not counting his money. Maybe he had a pension from the military, or some other stipend that made it possible to live on the wages of a rent-a-cop.

I nodded, I smiled. And so did Bill. I believed that at some juncture in his life Bill had made decisions he didn't know at the time he was making—that had won him medals or by which he'd let his comrades down . . . I'm sure I imagined too much, but I saw an old war not quite faded in his eyes.

This was what our imaginary conversations—that is, forgive me, *my* imaginary conversations—often touched on. The indiscernible points, the little dimes, where fate takes its sharpest turns. I explained no more to him than I did to anybody else, but he spoke freely of his life after this thing that had happened, or hadn't quite. Of how afterward he'd found it impossible to decide anything, or not to decide. How at a point in his journey out of mourning he'd wandered into a tunnel in which he traveled alone, and had no one to talk to, and couldn't call out. Because of the consequences, the split-second consequences, everything he did or didn't do became impossible.

And naturally, because I was talking to him in my head, the whole conversation was a monologue, and it was all about me. Exile, detachment, paralysis, fear—all the qualities people projected onto my flat white surface—they really played no part in anything that happened after the accident that took my wife and daughter. Everything occurred despite its complete impossibility. Including my decision, that day, to look for Heidi Franklin at the Art Department.

The doors to the Fine Arts Building lay directly across a paved court, almost a patio, that served the museum's entrance, too. By walking over this pavement in the freezing weather, by stepping outside the routines I'd set for myself and going to see a woman, I wasn't doing anything special, certainly not stirring my lifeless portions. I might have thought so three years earlier, when I'd still mistaken my paralysis for simple grief. But it wasn't simple.

The day of the accident, our neighbor picked up Anne and Elsie, my wife and daughter, out front of our house, and made a U-turn heading for the highway. I stopped them with a wave and leaned down to the driver's window. There'd been an ice storm the night before. The streets were dangerous. I thought he should take the gravel shortcut to town, I thought he should stay off the fast roads. He'd been pointed toward the shortcut anyway, and now he'd turned around. "Aren't you just heading on through to town?" "No, because of construction." "It's Sunday," I told the old man, "they won't be working."

Everybody knew our neighbor, General Neally, retired many years from the Air Force (and, incidentally, a widower), as a vigorous, tennis-playing, memoir-writing Southern gentleman. But lately he'd been getting frail, I thought. Once when I watched him heading in his Cadillac out of his driveway and pausing to look right and left, right and left, and again right and left, more confused, it seemed, than cautious, I wondered if he should have been operating a car. Only a couple of weeks before the accident, the General and I had met one morning at our mailboxes and he'd invited me to his kitchen for coffee. As he puttered around after the makings he grew silent and scratched his head, turned around to face me, and said in absolute surprise, "What do you want!"

All this was on my mind as I stood beside his car, failing even to glance at my family on the other side of him—I remember that often: I might have looked one last time into their faces, but didn't—and told the General, "Take the gravel road, it's shorter." "I like the big highway anyway," he said. And drove off. I stood there with one last statement—"Take the gravel road. It's safer"—on the tip of my tongue. On the tip of my tongue. I can still taste it in my mouth. If only I'd said it. Even if he'd again rejected my advice, he'd have been delayed a few more seconds during the exchange, and maybe they'd all be alive today. During the next few terrible weeks, imagination served up other things I could have done. I might have kept them home, or called them a cab, or kept our own car out of the shop another few days—it was only in for a tune-up, because of the warranty. I might have kept a second car . . . but we didn't need one, I commuted to the District each day in the Senator's limousine. So I said nothing, and they drove away.

Five miles down the road the General came to a stop sign, applied his brakes, and floated over the ice into the path of a panel truck going forty miles an hour. (A truck from a florist's shop. I don't know—I didn't view the scene—but I assume there were flowers everywhere.) At once Anne and Elsie were dead. The General survived for twenty-four hours, but never woke up. May they all rest in peace.

This winter day exactly four years later I went across the separating court, past the tarnished sculptures, through the doors of the Fine Arts Building. Went along through my tunnel, as I had for four years now. I took each step entirely out of a dull curiosity, not as to what waited ahead, because I didn't care, but as to whether or not I could take one more step. I hadn't found much else to interest me along the way. At the risk of stretching the illustration, I can say I sometimes came to turnings in the darkness and wondered if this were a labyrinth.

The Fine Arts Building was an old one, with high ceilings

that made the halls seem narrow and proportioned for some earlier, elongated race of academics. The place reeked of oils and glues and old wood. I didn't expect Heidi to be in. I thought I'd end up leaving a message at the office. A young man with a stubbly goatee, the rest of his head hairless, seemed to be in charge there. When I asked for Heidi Franklin he ducked behind his desk and was gone, entirely gone. "Excuse me?" I called. I stepped closer and peered over the desk to find him bent low over the floor, fiddling with the plug to his electric typewriter. "She might be at the performance," he said.

"Can I leave her a note?"

He stood up and I noticed a clever touch of style in his otherwise baggy contemporary apparel: a powder-blue Lacoste alligator shirt. Where the alligator patch belonged, the material was torn away and a small patch of his bare chest showed instead. A tiny alligator was tattooed there. "Try the Cannon Performance. Room Eight," he said.

"Cannon Performance? Sounds dangerous."

"I'm sure it's meant to."

I found Room Eight just a few steps down the hallway and peeked through the half-open door to see a number of students, say two dozen, most of them lounging on the floor, others perched on stools, all of them outfitted and decorated in the disheveled and expressive Art Department mode. Easels had been pushed aside and stools and chairs herded together. The large room was silent. But I couldn't see any performance, no one performing, though most of the front of the room lay visible to me. I stepped in quietly and sat at a wooden school desk by the entrance, more a part of the miscellany, the drop cloths and easels and boxes, than of the audience. Now I could see the room's near corner, and on a small platform a woman perched on a table with her legs widely parted, her left foot up beside her and the right one dangling, a young woman, nude below the waist except for her shoes—black tennies, high-top, unlaced, one lace purple or darkish and the other white or gray—engaged in shaving her lathered mons veneris. She used a pink disposable safety razor. I sat close enough to see these facts and colors. She was having some trouble with this operation, making very short strokes of her razor, swishing it vigorously in a chipped enamel bowl of water after every couple of strokes, and changing razors frequently from a plastic package full of them.

It took me a bit to recognize the young woman I'd met at Ted MacKey's the same night I'd met Heidi Franklin, that is, the tipsy cellist in the blue velvet dress. I tried to stay with the conventionally visible facts: She had red hair, pretty blue eyes, the faint violet circles around them more pronounced because of her complexion's paleness. At the moment she wore a yellow baseball cap and a blue T-shirt that said *Edgars* in white cursive letters across the breast.

I'd meant to sit out of the way, but as the dais was tucked into this corner, my corner, where I hadn't expected to find it, I was very nearly in the lap of the performer. Did freckles wander over her knees? As I leaned forward to see, I caught myself, terribly embarrassed. But nobody was looking at me. The students attended carefully, like the audience in an operating theater, with a collective attitude that seemed clinical if not outright jaded: She was an artist, that's all. I couldn't imagine why they called this a Cannon Performance.

Very close to me stood the teacher, a short, barrel-chested man in jeans and a red sweatshirt. He looked tough and loud, but right now he was wordless. Also I'm guessing he didn't feel very tough. I never met him, then or later, and was never able to ask.

As the session broke up—or at any rate as this performance was concluded with a wiping away of moist wisps of lather with a white hand towel, and she closed her legs and pulled down the hem of her blue T-shirt and sought about for her jeans with her free hand, laying the towel aside simultaneously, and others began to move around the room—I left. I went out to the court full of metal figures and walked from piece to piece, frowning so hard at them I eventually became aware of a pinpoint agony between my eyebrows. The sculptures seemed altogether leaden, unwieldy, pointless. And you'd better believe I'd forgotten all about Heidi Franklin.

Entirely out of habit, I walked off toward the School of Law. What had I witnessed? The point of the performance was lost on me but its effect was a wallop, and I stood by the skating pond clutching its cold railing with my bare hands, disoriented by the youth around me, not for the first time on this campus. The pond was covered by a cloud rising off the ice, the island in the middle of it almost invisible. And ominous. A looming arrival, a ghostly advent, the ghost ship of mariners' legends.

For half an hour I stood and watched these young skaters and tried to put them together with what I'd just seen. But the attempt itself was an act of minor hysteria. A Cannon Performance? I certainly felt shot by a cannonball.

Here before me was another vivid picture—youth, freshness, vigor, the very life-breath visible out of their mouths—the cinematic picture, coming toward me out of the fog, growing substantial and then astonishing. Bright colors, breaths and words and laughter and the skirl of their blades, and then they faded, they were nothing. Yet on the other hand these same youngsters seemed to illustrate not life and youth and games, but training. All in a line and a direction, drilling for the march. The faces changed, but the round went on, and the round brought to mind the slave's drawing that so affected me, the line pursuing its model until it was no longer a failed emulation, no longer an unintended parody, but finally an abomination of ignorance.

I myself was hunched like a skater, still gripping the railing, and I was filled, suddenly, with a sense of rightness and truth—flooded and becalmed in the wake of an insight: I recognized that every one of these skaters wore my face.

For precisely four years I'd hovered like this around my own past. A ghost moving in the mist. Circling, attending, ministering to the great beshrouded monolith. And coming back to the slave's drawing almost daily, as a disfigured actor might be drawn repeatedly to the mystery of his face in the mirror. Now its lesson came clear: As I followed my own round over and over I wandered farther and farther from its core, my course less and less beholden to the central shape. For a long time now I'd really had little to do with the source of my grief. I was in fact quite free of it. Yet my devotion remained.

Nothing was required of me. I just had to put one foot in front of the other, and one day I'd wander wide enough of my dark cold sun to break gently from my orbit.

I belted my overcoat, but with difficulty, my hands senseless by now with cold. I twisted my scarf under my chin and pulled on my gloves. I turned away from this revelation and toward the world, hungry to get the news about myself. What would happen to me now?

I can't say this next thought simply occurred to me, because in fact it stayed with me constantly. It surfaced now as it often did, that's all: In a few more years my daughter would have gone to college. I would have loved for her to whirl to a stop by this railing and laugh the sweet laughter of old movies on television. Above all I would have loved for Elsie to have turned out something like . . . but I couldn't remember the cellist's name.

My eagerness stayed fresh for a while, a few days, better than a week. Then, oppressed by low gray clouds, low temperatures, it faded. But I waited.

A breath of change in late February gave over to a succession of blizzards in early March. The meteorologists couldn't help themselves and repeated the phrase "blanketing the Midwest" over and over. The town took on the breadlike curvatures of Alpine villages in photographs. The skaters went away. The skating pond, and even its railing, disappeared beneath several feet of snow. The red sculptures at the top of the monolith went under, too. Roofs imploded, vehicles and livestock were buried, travel stopped, everybody suffered, and we were well into April before the skies cleared and the white fields began to thaw.

The weather defeated all of us. With the difficulties, the delays, everyone fell behind. By the time I got around to visiting J. J. Stein at the Forum for Interpretative Scholarship, I thought it possible he'd forgotten we'd ever met.

I'd never before seen the Forum grounds, an odd piece of our University settled a dozen miles outside of town, in a compound that had been an insane asylum in the days when they were called exactly that. This day of my visit to the Swan's Grove Campus the weather felt new. Winter's edges had been pushed back, the sidewalks were clear and the roads were dry. The deep snow in the fields had collapsed into dimples that had become, at last, here and there, craters with soaked gray pasture at their bottoms.

"The Grove," as J. J. Stein called it, was one of those academic backwaters into which state money miraculously and secretly finds its way, the kind of place some enterprising state legislator, I thought, would someday expose and ruin. As if to protect the place from attacks on its irrelevance, the University Hospital ran its small Head Trauma Rehabilitation Unit out here. Also, in one of the old buildings once full of madness, a charitable foundation housed a printing press. Dr. J.J.'s Forum for Interpretive Scholarship had a small L-shaped structure to itself.

He showed me all around the grounds, steering me by the arm as if I were decrepit. Others were out taking the air as well. Some of them looked drunk, probably patients from the Rehabilitation Unit. We toured the grove of elms that gave the place its name, the various buildings, the creek, the handball court. None of this was necessary. We just wanted to stroll in the wet sunshine.

Coming up from under the terrible winter, it all looked dismal. Ripe for haunting. Colossal, unwieldy crows congregated in the bare branches of the elms. "Seventeen acres," J.J. said. "It was bought in the thirties for nothing. The College of Medicine did experiments out here on animals for several decades. That big smokestack is the crematorium." He pointed to a hundred feet of brick rising out of a small concrete structure. We were crossing the central field diagonally, using a wide paved walk. "They've still got a facility over by the creek. Most of us stay away from it."

Plainly the place's creepy history was much enjoyed by some of the people who used it now. J.J. brightened as he talked about it, although none of the folks we crossed paths with seemed to be enjoying anything much, and many put me in mind of the former denizens. In the strangeness of spring, finally without hats, our jackets open, inhaling the warm air suspiciously, I'm sure we all looked like lunatics. It didn't help that some of us staggered or shuffled, wearing open galoshes and pajamas under overcoats, practicing simple movements with rehabilitated heads.

Just such a person as I've described blocked our path—

a smiling man with one hand raised high above his head—and said to me, "I'd like to give you my address."

J.J. spoke up and said, "That's fine. But do we need your address?"

The man leaned unsteadily to one side as if fighting a strong wind, his left hand raised and the fingers curled around an imaginary baton, or a small invisible torch. "I'd like to give you my address."

"Okay," I said. "Go ahead, if you want."

"I'd like to give you my address," the man said. "I'd like to give you my address."

He stood before us for a while with an expectant and inquiring slant to his eyebrows, as if the next move were ours. As we walked around him, he continued on his way with his left hand held aloft.

After J.J. had shown me the grounds and everything else, the offices available to such as me, the copying facilities and coffee lounge and rest rooms, introduced me to Mrs. Towne, the gray-headed secretary in the flowered dress who served all the Forum members (but I saw no Forum members; the place was a morgue), after this short tour, he invited me into his office, sat us both in chairs, put his feet up on his desk, and said, "We don't have anything for you, I'm afraid."

"Well," I said, feeling stupid, irritated, and relieved. I really didn't want to work here anyhow, not unless I was shooting a horror film. "It's certainly been a pleasure looking the place over."

He brushed this off and started a long explanation about

funding and so on that almost started to interest me, or rather his discomfort and his unexpected and charming inability to handle it did.

"Look, Michael," he said finally, getting up. "I'm bullshitting you. It's the politics. The Foundation people are all affluent lefties. You had to work for Senator Thom!"

I laughed and said, "I didn't have to."

And he said, "Michael, I could use a friend. Let me take you to dinner."

I hesitated too long. He must have known I was hunting for an alibi.

"My divorce is final today," he said.

I'd heard about it. His wife, a campus beauty, had been pursued and seduced by a visiting author, the famous novelist T. K. Nickerson. She'd managed the final details of the divorce from the flat she and the author shared these days in Rome.

"Okay. Let's get a bite," I said.

I left J.J. to close up his shop and walked alone out under a supernatural cloudscape, the sunset soaking the underbellies of huge formations. The entire world was pink. While I waited out front, a man came toward me, the same one who'd stopped us a while earlier, still gripping some tall invisible thing in the pastel dusk. With his free hand he offered me a piece of paper. "Here. This is my address. It's written down here."

"Is this you? Robert Hicks?"

"Check. Robert Hicks," he said. "What's your name?"

"Mike."

"Mike what?"

"Reed."

"Reed what?"

"Michael Reed. That's my name."

"Check. Michael Reed," he said.

"Who are these other people?" On the scrap of typesheet he'd handed me, a list of almost a dozen names followed his own.

"Those are my friends in the Unit. The Head Trauma Rehabilitation Unit," he said, "check, the H-T-R-U."

"Oh."

"We all have the same address. Check."

"I get it."

"The H-T-R-U. The H-T-R-U. The H-T-R-U," Robert Hicks said.

"Robert—does anybody ever ask you what you're holding?"

"Not too much. Once in a while."

"And what is it?"

"I don't know. I can't see it. It's very light," he said.

He started talking to himself loudly in words I couldn't understand, and walked away.

I sat on a bus-stop bench, the same stop the campus shuttle had let me out at when I'd arrived, because I didn't own an automobile, and I watched the aimless strollers—so many of whom had been rendered permanently aimless by bad accidents—as many as two dozen people out on the grounds, concentrating hard on going nowhere. I was convinced I could pick out the patients, the ones getting better, from the University con artists

3

like myself trudging among the buildings. But the new air, the pink sunset, the wide pocked field of slush crossed by the gray bars of the sidewalks like a big faded Confederate flag, people marching crookedly over it as if the battle had just ended . . . it wouldn't be claiming too much to say that as I sat there holding in my fingers Mr. Hicks's list of head-injury victims I felt the stirring even of parts of me that had been dead since childhood, that sense of the child as a sort of antenna stuck in the middle of an infinite expanse of possibilities. And childhood's low-grade astonishments, its intimations of a perpetual circus . . . meeting, at random, kids with small remarkable talents or traits, with double-jointed thumbs, a third or even a fourth set of teeth. I don't claim I enjoyed those long-ago days very much, they were so full of ridiculous horrors, but there was also this capacity of the universe to delight by turning up, like a beautiful shell on a long empty beach, a kid whose older teenaged sister liked to show off her bare breasts, or a boy who could take a drag off a cigarette, pinch his mouth and nostrils shut, and force smoke out through his ears. What happened to them? The boy whose hands were an optical illusion. His hands looked reasonably pro-portioned and complete, they were unremarkable until you looked closely and discovered that each hand had only three fin-gers, plus a thumb. But if you asked me, "Which finger was missing?" I couldn't have chosen. All his fingers seemed to be there.

"Are you looking at my hands?" J.J. asked me on the drive into town. I'd been staring at his two-fisted grip on the wheel of his Karmann Ghia.

I told him about the boy I'd known. "That's interesting," he said, but I think he meant it was a stupid thing to admit having on your mind. Meanwhile I suspected his own mind was on his divorce. He seemed preoccupied, and we didn't talk much as he drove the rattling sports car into town. As we got out of his car in a deserted parking ramp, he told me, "My hands are normal . . ." I heard an implied "*But,*" and thought he'd now proceed to introduce me to some grotesque secret about his body. Instead he locked his classic car from the outside, using the key in both doors, and led me to dinner.

There were the troughs where students ate pizza or ribs or burgers or stir-fry, and then there were the establishments that had erected price barriers against all youth, where you could sit and talk. J.J. took us to one of the quiet ones, a small Italian place dedicated to romance. We sat by a frosty window—right after sunset the air had turned chilly—at a table for two spread with checkered linen. We were early. A waiter went around lighting candles shoved into Chianti bottles. I waited for J.J. to talk about his sadness, but instead, while we drank the house wine and waited for the food, he asked me about Senator Thom. "I'm curious—I'm trying to pin you down," he admitted. "Did you like the guy or hate him? Did you quit or get fired?"

"Finally. Someone crass enough to ask."

"You're not slapping my hand, are you?"

"No. Really. Nobody's ever asked."

"It's just that he's in the news right now. I saw him last night on the tube, dueling with journalists."

Questions about the Senator's ethics had come before the public recently. Not for the first time. "'Fight every battle on TV,'" I quoted. "One of his mottoes. He's got a million."

J.J. said, "Many predict the end of his career."

"Not me."

"Did you accomplish anything? Working for him?"

"In D.C. I experienced what I once heard called 'the temptation to be good.' It's a curse. As soon as it hit me I got confused. I still don't know if, by quitting, I gave in to a bad temptation, or managed to resist a good one."

"Wow. Sounds like Zen," he said. "Am I supposed to make sense of it?"

"There's a perfect stillness at the center of Washington," I said, and he folded his hands before him with the pleasant air of someone stuck beside a psycho on a public bus. "It's natural to talk about it in paradoxes," I insisted. "Everything in the world is going on there, but nothing's happening. It's all essential, but it's all completely pointless. The motives are virtuous, but whatever you do just stinks. And then you retire with great praise."

"Well, we sort of guess all that, don't we? So why did you enlist?"

"I've got a half-dozen explanations," I said, "but I'll give you the shortest one: It was financial. I was restless, and I was curious, but mainly I was just poor. I wanted to leave behind the pinchpenny life of a high-school teacher. The prospect of money somewhere down the line meant a lot to me."

"But you didn't get it."

"I got a raise."

"But you didn't get rich."

"No."

"And you don't care."

"No. Not right now. Should I?"

"No," he said. Then: "How much of a raise?"

"I went from the low thirties to—after two or three years—just about eighty thousand. Just under."

"Hey. That's not bad!"

"I was designated executive legal staff. That put me at the high end."

"And how are your politics now? Or am I prying?"

"You mean, will I vote for Senator Thom?" The Controversial Senator Tom-Tom, he was called by his constituents. The Big Chief, he was also called. I had stayed with the Senator at first in the hope of having influence, later in the hope of being there on the day of his defeat, finally in the hope of gathering evidence to bring him down. But he was clean, and it wouldn't be fair to omit saying that he was even a good man. It's just that his principles were small and his horizon was November. He should have been a Republican, but he was a Democrat—why? Why not? I think very little of either party now, and I can't understand how I ever managed to see any difference between them. Worst of all, somewhere in the middle of my visit to that planet, I'd misplaced my sense of humor about all this. Would I vote for Senator Thom?

"I no longer vote," I told J.J.

The spaghetti and the lasagna came. J.J. changed the subject, wanted to know how I felt about teaching, about students, about the academy. And now I got it—he was conducting an interview after all.

How many interviews, how many J.J.s winding what quantity of pasta around how many forks, did the future hide? The question dropped me in a pit. Is there any limit, I thought, to how boring this place can be? By the time we'd both turned down dessert and were halfway through our cups of coffee, I'd decided no. No limit. "Do you know what?" I said. "I think I'll let this next year be my last. I believe I'm through with the life of the mind." Getting it said felt like a minor thing, but necessary. Like finally taking a second to tie a flapping shoelace.

"Through with the life of the mind! Now I'm convinced you're just the guy we need at the Forum."

"No. Thanks, but no."

A bit of silence between us now. We heard a man and a woman talking at the table just next to ours. The woman mentioned somebody's funeral. J.J. took an interest.

He stopped eating. He was clearly eavesdropping. Now the woman said, "I think it's muggy in Alabama. Isn't it?"

"Muggy?" the man said. "It's Alabama."

"I'm sorry," J.J. said, "excuse me—"

They both looked over at us.

J.J. said to them, "Trevor Watt is dead?"

They looked at each other for a second, and then back at J.J. "Yes—he's dead." It came out of both their mouths at once.

The man said, "He had a heart attack last Saturday."

J.J. cleared his throat. He looked stunned. "I'm sorry," he said again. "He was a pretty good acquaintance of mine. Where was he?"

"He was at Brown," the woman said.

The man said, "Well, but he'd retired. He was living in—"

"Down in Alabama someplace," the woman said.

While we paid our bill, J.J. went on chatting with them, and I urged him to take his time. I stepped outside and stood smoking a cigar on the sidewalk. Casually I drop that fact, but actually I've never smoked. This one had been given to me. People gave me gifts, people liked me, maybe because they sensed I was virtually dead and couldn't hurt them.

I'd been waiting for J.J to take up the subject of his wife, to open a window on his bitterness this day of his divorce. But nothing of the kind had happened. He and his wife had been separated a couple of years. Crossing the legal finish line seemed to have made him pensive today, but I supposed in general he'd mended.

As a matter of fact, just a few weeks previous I'd met J.J.'s wife. This was at a large dinner party at a Dean's house, one of those old-fashioned affairs where many had come for dinner but most—the students—would be booted out after cocktails. She'd been traveling through with T. K. Nickerson, the writer who'd won her away from us. Everybody called him "Kit." Her name was Kelly. Kit and Kelly had been on their way to, or from, Europe in the dead of winter. Kelly was a beautiful woman, striking without having to be glamorous. She just dropped a purple silk dress over her head and she was ready to spend an evening in a room full of men trying not to go crazy in her presence. Tiberius Soames, my Haitian colleague in the Department of History, attached himself to her early that evening and never left her side. Her eyes looked sleepy, but her gaze was vibrant. She had very pale eyelashes. Straight strawberry hair to her shoulders.

Another redhead was also there at the dinner party that night, the redheaded cellist, the creator of the Cannon Performance, that is. She was working for the caterer of this affair, helping in the kitchen and bringing around the food. She wore a gray-and-white uniform and had her hair bunched under a black net, and she looked very plain. But that only accentuated the aura of her mischief. She moved among us with a tray like the secret queen of some criminal enclave, casing the joint. As I reached for one of her hors d'oeuvres, she smiled and said, "Hello, Michael Reed."

It had been a month or so since we'd met at Ted MacKey's, and then only briefly. Tonight I'd noticed her right away, but I hadn't expected to be remembered. I was astonished. I probably looked it. She smiled and passed by.

Before we all sat down to eat, I made sure to find out her name. This was a nerve-racking endeavor, not entirely to my surprise. Less than two weeks earlier, I'd been staring at her naked privates. I tried to intersect her path as if by accident. I sidled around and we approached each other at a drift, like objects in outer space. "You're overly fond of these little numbers," she said of the items on her tray.

"No. I was trying to remember your name. I'm sorry. I can't remember."

"Flower." After a small challenging beat of silence during which I managed not to ask if she was kidding, she said, "Yes. Flower Cannon."

"Oh!—Cannon."

"Oh?"

"I must not have heard it, back when we met."

"You'd have remembered."

"Yes."

"But you saw one of my performances last month, I think."

"Well," I said.

"Did you like it?"

"Well . . ." But I was stalled. I'd become completely stupid. "That is the full text of my remarks," I said.

Flower Cannon laughed at me and moved along.

As for Kelly Stein, J.J.'s wife, I didn't pass one word with her beyond a glancing introduction, because during dinner she sat way down the long board, in another conversational district.

I sat almost directly facing Kit Nickerson, however: a much less formidable figure than the black-and-white portraits on his book flaps, a tall and thin man with a boxer's mashed nose, a prominent Adam's apple, and kind, watery eyes. He had a bit of a stutter. But it went away as he began arguing with a young author who sat across the table and a couple of places down, so that their exchange roped in a small audience of several others of us. It was hard not to feel slightly embarrassed for the other fellow, a guest teacher in the English Department here, as Kit himself had been two years before, when he'd hooked up with Kelly Stein—a prodigy of sorts, this much younger man, still in his twenties, half lost in his baggy clothing, with shoulder-length hair and a sweet face that cleared him of any suspicion, at least it seemed to me, that he liked to pick fights. "Do you want me to lie?" Kit asked him. "Because I could certainly manage it. Lying is sort of my vocation." That was the first audible remark.

Apparently the younger man had accused the famous novelist of betraying his early promise. How he'd reached such a point in the middle of a lot of small talk would have been hard to trace, but having found himself out here past the glow of the party's lights, so to speak, out in the dark with the great man, he wasn't backing down, give him that much. I saw his fingers trembling as he touched his water glass. He succeeded in keeping his gaze direct. "The people in your early books were all different from each other. You really sampled the world. I mean, those characters, like in *Quest for Tears,* or any of the early ones, really . . . they have *some* commonalities, they're people who all have at least some education, and real passion, but outside of that, they can belong to any class, any walk of life. I mean, you got around, put it that way. Now it's just people covered in jewels, people on yachts, people at state dinners . . . I'm sorry, I mean I say this as an admirer, a follower, an emulator even—but don't you think you're turning into sort of a lap-dog for the privileged?"

"But Seth," Kit said, "you're just being a snob in reverse. Don't privileged people have feelings, too? Don't they have inner lives? Can't their passion be real?"

"There's more to it than their material circumstances. Nowadays—in your books nowadays—somehow they're kind of morally—uh." He was wilting. "Morally aloof."

"Uh-oh! Wait a minute!"

"That sounds stupid. Maybe I don't know what I mean." Seth shook his head, embarrassed.

"No. No. Please. Don't chicken out. What *do* you mean? Why should this accusation prick me?"

"Or, okay, I'll say the characters are morally unin*struc*-tive—"

"Hey, come on, Seth. They're fictional. Do you really hope to get your moral lessons from people who don't exist?"

"You don't challenge them to get down in the muck of themselves and find out what's right and what's wrong. Not like you used to—like you once did."

Kit, who seemed in general a charming man, became at this moment, while his admirer tried to explain himself, suddenly very unattractive, somehow elongated and parsonlike. One corner of his mouth twitched with cartoonish villainy, I have to say, as if he'd arrived first all by himself at this dinner party and set traps around the place and Seth had just sprung one. And the kid did have the nauseated look of someone dangling upside down.

"Look," Kit said. "You talk about my books as if they're artifacts. Maybe yours are. Maybe your books are artifacts and maybe for you they serve as currency in various transactions I can't guess about because I don't know you. It's up to you to decide whether those transactions are corrupt or not. I can't accuse you." But he said this as if he was in fact leveling some sort of accusation that none of us, nobody other than Seth himself, could understand. I think it was just a conversational ploy, and I don't think Seth understood the charge any more than the rest of us. It was just that Kit had been in this corner before and he knew how to duel his way out of it without having to say anything that actually made sense.

Having leaned across the table to get right in the guy's face and put this sinister turn on the conversation, he sat back.

Seth said, "My *book* . . . there's only one, and I don't know if it's really worth talking about."

"Then we won't talk about your book." By now the whole table was silent, and as he clearly sensed he'd sounded too harsh a note, Nickerson limped on. "Andrew, Andrew, my books aren't *artifacts*. They're sloughed off behind me like dead skins. They're organic to the life."

"Well . . . okay, I guess." Seth didn't have quite enough steel left now to tell him his name wasn't Andrew.

The table was silent. Kit's gaze drifted toward Kelly's end, maybe seeking some touchstone of support. It stopped at Tiberius Soames, who looked bloated with emotion, in fact whose face in the candlelight seemed to change size and shape rapidly. Soames managed to say: "Dead *skins*." He coughed violently several times, sighed with exasperation, looked away from us, from all of this. "Dead skins!"

"They're detritus," Nickerson said of his books.

This was right around the end of the meal, whether before or after dessert I can't remember. Whenever the liqueur is served. I happened to glance in through the briefly open kitchen door where Joan, Mrs. Martin Peele, wife of the Dean of Liberal Arts and the woman of the house, consulted with Eloise, who catered almost all the faculty dinners. Eloise was a character, a very small, rapid woman, perpetually sardonic, and always smoking. She had a round Peter Lorre face and a thin-lipped Peter Lorre mouth. All she needed in this world was a foot-long holder for her cigarette. Mrs. Peele looked flushed and happy. Geniuses were fighting at her party. Directly behind our hostess's back, Flower Cannon tilted a jug of what looked like Drambuie to her mouth, gulped down a quick one, exhaled, and set the bottle on a tray. I believed she was looking right at me. I expected her to wink. But she didn't.

Sixteen of us surrounded the dregs of the meal at a long wooden trestle table without a tablecloth. The floor and the walls around us were also of wood, all of it brilliantly finished and gleaming as if this room had just emerged from under a rain cloud. For a few long seconds I stopped bothering to hear—sometimes this happens to me—and just observed how the group of us sat in a big, wet place.

"So, okay," Kit Nickerson went on, "okay. I hope I've got books out ahead of me that do the work you're asking for, but I have to live my way *to* them, and *through* them. That's what

I mean when I say they're not artifacts. There's no turning back, that's for sure. I can't reassume my former shape. Put it like that." Now he sat back farther, relaxing, and let us all off the hook by addressing everybody so that we were no longer spectators at what in Washington we'd always called a pissing contest or a dick-off. "They aren't incidental, unimportant— I'm not saying they're garbage—listen, I know they're books, I know I've made them, I hope they're beautiful. But I have to leave them behind me as I move along the life."

"There's no looking back," Seth agreed. "Like Emerson— 'Say what you think today in hard words, and if you have to, contradict it tomorrow in words just as hard.'"

Everybody was relieved to hear him arguing Kit's side of it now, as Flower and Eloise came around with three liqueurs.

"*Exactement!*" Kit said. "Let's drink to it!"

Maybe the celebrated author took such criticism more seriously than I give him credit for, because later, while people sat around the table, having broken up into tiny conversations, he still wasn't finished, though Seth was—Seth had left. "Well," Kit said to a couple of us, "I might be an old hack . . . At least I'm not an old hack with nothing better to do than imitate his earlier stuff. The ground I break might not be new to everybody else, but it's new to me, and that's how I keep myself interested." He paused. "And if you don't get your hand off my woman's knee," he told Tiberius Soames, "I'm going to knock your head out from between your ears."

Soames looked bored. He repeated his previous remark: "Dead *skins*," he said.

He was dressed in a white single-breasted suit with wide lapels and vivid burgundy stripes and looked like a Mississippi minstrel. All night he'd managed to be quietly, yet wildly, inappropriate. This was just at the start of March, two months after his stint in the psychopathic ward.

As I left that night, a bit early so as to avoid the others, I reflected that even if I hadn't liked Kit Nickerson's performance very much I still had to agree with him, particularly from the perspective of advanced middle age, about the dangers of imitating oneself, repeating old moves, clinging to routines and rituals long after they've stopped holding us up, and we're holding them up instead. About the danger in hiding oneself away from the nauseating vastness of a conscious human life. I was excited, glad I'd come tonight, glad I'd come to the University in the first place.

I looked back toward the lighted kitchen window and I saw Eloise the caterer with her face tilted up, laughing and exhaling a cloud of smoke. Of Flower Cannon I saw only her back and shoulders as she swayed in her gray outfit, wiping down the kitchen counter.

Now, outside the Italian restaurant, by calling back the scene into my mind's eye, I managed to conjure one almost exactly like it: a solitary moment in the dark, a warm window . . . and now, right now, as I puffed experimentally on my big Churchill, the woman herself, Flower Cannon, appeared before me in a cloud of cigar smoke.

I stood on a pedestrian walkway. The walkway passed between two buildings, a hotel and a boutique. Framed in a tall ground-floor office window of the hotel was Flower Cannon. She sat in a swivel chair before a computer console, apparently daydreaming at her task, arching back with a weary air, her right arm limp and distended, dangling a pen.

In my head I talked to her as much as I did anybody else, as much as Bill the museum man, even more. You, I told her. You act wild and it's not fake. You have a kind of blessed ignorance. You are California. What do I mean you are California? I asked her. You're long and your variousness sweeps down to the Pacific Ocean. There's no reason not to say these things when nobody's listening.

Tapping on the glass seemed wrong: I'd only have succeeded in troubling her, probably—a figure in an alley, tapping. On the other hand, that figure was pretty much who I was.

I went around to the building's entrance to see if I could find her and say hello. The lobby was polished wood and brass—luxurious, silent. I was alone. Not even a concierge or a night clerk. From the front desk I could see back into the office now, where she sat beside her vague reflection in the window.

It was somebody else entirely, a woman quite a bit blonder and with a face deeply tanned for this time of year, working late, taking a minute for her thoughts. It wasn't Flower Cannon.

I stared at her until a man who appeared to have no function whatsoever here approached me and said, "Sir, we'd rather you didn't smoke inside the lobby."

A light sleet was falling as I came out of the hotel. I stepped backward under the awning and watched out for J.J. I thought about my wife. Whereas before I'd chased away any memories of her, now I found myself catching at what I could, and it was less and less. Anne drank a lot of black coffee. She liked cinnamon-spiced chewing gum. Anne was thin, intelligent, humorous, sweet. She fidgeted. She cleared her throat a lot. She frowned when something struck her as funny. Human stupidity tickled her, she wore the world lightly, and that was important to me. I needed her. In the heights and depths, in the most silly and trivial ways, she was my wife. And now here was Flower Cannon.

I wouldn't say I was infatuated. I had noticeable but manageable feelings for her, helpless lustful feelings, and fatherly feelings, and the mild resentful envy of someone no longer young for someone so full of vitality. Feelings not at all different in kind from those I entertained for every young woman in the world—different however in degree; stronger.

Women had always appeared fair to my eyes. Yes, college girls, and even the high-school girls I once taught. But much of that evaporated when I became a father to my own little girl. Now every woman looked like somebody's daughter. And after I lost her, they all began to look like my own daughter—to look like Elsie, inhabiting her years, filled with my daughter's unlived life, Elsie seeking something out of their eyes.

Curious to say, her name wasn't Elizabeth, or anything else to do with Elsie. She was Huntley, a name arguably a lot nicer, but as a baby she had a stuffed animal—these days they call them "sleeping animals"—named Elsie by the manufacturers, and labeled Elsie across her bearish belly. In that world, in the baby's crib, in that epoch, identities flowed back and forth. There weren't even fantasies then—all was fantasy. Through a kind of enchantment the child Huntley appropriated Elsie the bear's name, and kept it. The bear kept it, too. Everybody ended up Elsie, all the sleeping animals, also Anne. And for a little while even I was Elsie.

Everything became Elsie, and in a manner of speaking everything still is. In losing Anne I'd lost the woman in my life. But in losing Elsie, I'd lost all of us.

"Mike?" It was J.J., standing in front of the Italian place looking right and left and pulling on a pair of gloves. "He arrives!" he said to me. I went carefully down the slick steps.

Now, in this season of return, I felt myself becoming less and less Elsie and more and more Mike Reed. Less the man who'd lost his family, and more just somebody who didn't happen to have one.

"It's funny," J.J. said, the sleet landing and melting on his shoulders, "Trevor Watt was a teacher of mine, my most important teacher. For a while he was the most important person in my life. I mean, you know, I pored over every nuance. Do you know how it can be with a teacher, and you're young, you've got nothing yet, only what he confers on you? Every word he said was gold. Then suddenly I hated him. He betrayed all my worship. He didn't mean to. He just turned out to be human. And I burned with hatred for the guy. I wanted him dead. And when those people tonight mentioned his name, and now he *is* dead . . . I suddenly realized I hadn't thought of him since . . . I couldn't even tell you. It's been years."

When J.J. dropped me at my house, I didn't invite him inside. I made no excuse, though he actually got out and walked me to the door. We stood listening to the noise of a party across the street, students, surely, exploding after their midterms: a repeatedly banging screen door, and laughter, and the thump, thump, thump of their music.

J.J. jammed his gloved hands into the pockets of his leather jacket and said, "Ah! Youth."

A white car, one from the early seventies, a big old Moby Dick of an automobile, whizzed around the corner onto our block, blew a front tire with a cheerful plopping noise, and went into a pirouette that ended with the rear wheels on the sidewalk, where they spun angrily until they found a purchase and the vehicle shot into the street again, then stalled. Apparently satisfied with this as a final position, as a parking place, very nearly in the middle of this dead-end street, two young men got out with deliberate movements and stumbled toward the house where the others laughed.

J.J. said, "Hey—fellas—excuse me—"

They wandered on inside, and he shouted louder, "Hey!" and then screamed, "HEY—" and stopped himself.

For a few seconds we were silent. The noise of the party went on unabated. "I wouldn't want to repeat my younger days," I said, trying to sound sympathetic.

"Ah, well," he said. He smiled. In the light of streetlamps tears shone in his eyes. "I'm off," he said. "Thanks for the company."

"Any time. Really." I thought it very possible we'd see more of each other, two single men.

The ticking sound of the frozen rain stopped an hour or so after it started. The party down the block careened on through the night. For better than two years now this generally quiet section of town had been my neighborhood. I had an entire small house to myself. I slept in an attic bedroom. I kept the window wide open because it was always warm up there. The street dead-ended at some railway tracks, but apparently there were more important routes through town, because we hardly ever heard a train go by.

I lay in bed under the low ceiling and listened to the party across the street as the music got lower, as the number of voices diminished, although the voices themselves carried more clearly as the night grew deeper. Along about three in the morning I was wakened by shouts in the street.

"SEND OUT YOUR WOMEN!"

"SEND OUT YOUR WOMEN!"

They made this request over and over and over. A couple of young men, from the sound of them, maybe the same two young men who'd sailed on three tires down the middle of the neighborhood. They screamed for a good half hour, taking turns mostly, sometimes hollering simultaneously but by no means in unison, catching their breath and laughing and talking together, and then starting up again:

"SEND—OUT—YOUR—WOMEN!"

"SEND! OUT! YOUR! WOMEN!"

"SEND!—OUT!—" until they were hoarse.

This performance brought on the full spring. Over the next few weeks the students put melted-looking divans on the porches of their rooming houses, threw away their books and shoes, and got out their guitars. You could sit by an open window in the dusk and hear their whoops and laughter like the cries of wildlife. They were forever flitting over the flat dead lawns uncovered by the thaw, tossing baseballs, Frisbees, water balloons. They lay by the river in pairs, drove slowly down the streets in open convertibles playing loud rap music, like old-time loudspeaker trucks advertising humanity's least attractive secrets. I enjoyed all this. I liked the young students. I think my first spring here, they saved my life.

I saw Flower Cannon again at the end of April. The weather was warm. By noon of this particular day I was down to jeans and a T-shirt, carrying my sports coat over my shoulder. The people along the avenue seemed relaxed and alive. A combo of five students played jazz in a tiny garden park. There were children on the grass. Balloons were for sale. A snapshot would have caught mouths open in laughter and dogs floating in mid-air.

The two men who ran a shoeshine stand at the local bus station had moved their bench out onto the sidewalk. I climbed up onto one of the chairs there and presented my old walking boots. In airports and hotels the professionals generally refused to have a go at these clodhoppers, because

I'd worked the leather full of waterproofing compound. But these two, a white-headed old black man and his partner, who might have been his son or even his grandson, always cordially wiped them down and slapped some drops of oil on them.

"I guess they won't take a polish," I said, as I'd said to them many times over the last four years.

"That's all right," the old man said. "We can clean them up just as good as anything with some saddle soap and mink oil today."

The younger man took care of me while I sat in the elevated chair with my feet on the metal rests, watching the folks go by.

The old man, who'd been gone inside the station a while on some errand or other, returned and began sweeping down the area with a short broom, bent over in his navy pants and navy sweater. He seemed lost in a world of his own until he addressed his partner. "You tell him?"

"No."

"I'll go ahead and tell him then."

The other said nothing.

"That stuff you buy," he said to me, "it's just as good if you get a big jar of Vaseline. That's only what they use anyway. Vaseline petroleum jelly."

"Oh," I said, "you mean the waterproofing stuff."

"Yes. It's just Vaseline petroleum jelly. That's all you need to get. Or anything like that."

"Yeah. Okay."

"You might as well just get you a big jar," the old man said, "the large economy size. Be done with it."

"Be done with it," the young man said.

"What I want to know," the first said, "is how can he go every weekend over to the river, lose thirteen, fourteen hundred dollars, come on back like it was nothing."

"Yeah. Yeah. I don't know for sure," the other said.

I looked from one to the other and gathered they weren't talking about me.

"Go for a weekend, lose three thousand dollars like it wasn't nothing at all."

"He getting it somewhere."

"Three thousand, four thousand," the old man said. "He goes every weekend."

"He getting it from the A-rab."

"He don't never win. He go to the river, he lose a lot of money."

"Uh huh. Uh huh. Uh huh. I know," the younger said with considerable assurance.

"There's the river bus right now."

"Is it Eddie?"

"Naw. Eddie don't drive that river bus no more. Eddie's got a sister . . ."

"He got a sister? Eddie?" The younger man was finished with my boots now. He tapped each twice with the heel of his brush and pulled my cuffs down.

"Yeah. He got a sister . . . Now: you get in some water," the old man said to me. "Go ahead, stand up to your cuffs, your feet gonna be as dry as the desert. That's that woman driver driving today," he said to his partner. "See her?"

"Yeah. I see her."

"She's down in Chicago," he said.

"She is?"

I gave him ten dollars.

"That's why he driving down in Illinois now," he said.

"Go ahead and keep the change," I told him.

"Thank you very much," he said to me. *"Her,"* he told the other. *"Her,* I'm saying. Eddie's sister."

I left them to feel their way through a forest of pronouns and approached the woman driver of the bus to Riverside. She sat hunched over her big flat steering wheel examining a notebook as I looked up at her through the open door.

I had a twenty in my fingers. "Can I just pay you and get on and ride?" I asked.

"That's exactly how it works," she said.

I got on board.

"I don't need a ticket?"

"I got tickets. And they got tickets inside." She made change. "And you can order tickets through the mail. The whole world wants to sell you a ticket on my bus."

The bus was almost full of passengers, many of them probably going to the casino in Riverside. I sat next to a tiny old gentleman wearing sunglasses like the black bulging eyes of an insect. Across the aisle sat a small boulder of a man who revealed to me, as soon as the bus had swung onto the interstate highway out of town, that he played blackjack in

Riverside several times a month; that his name was Vince; that until hard work had worn out his joints he'd made his living principally as a Sheetrocker, but now he survived on government disability checks supplemented by his natural good luck. Once he had my attention Vince kept talking, looking deeply into my face. Meanwhile where the tiny old man looked, from behind his black orbs, nobody knew. I understood that poker players often wore sunglasses to keep their emotions secret. I sensed he was being stoic about something enormous.

Getting aboard this bus had been a crazy impulse, but I'd actually been meaning to go to Riverside for some time now. A musician by the name of Smokey Henderson, a trumpeter who led a jazz trio and whom I'd met through Ted Mackey, had told me that as a regular thing his group played in a club attached to the Indian casino there. I'd enjoyed their music at Ted's house once or twice, and it just seemed like the right kind of day to go looking for more of it.

Riverside lay forty-five miles out along the two-lane black-top known around these parts as the Old Highway. I'd been told it was a quiet town, part of the reservation along the Sioux River.

I was expected later that afternoon at a small gathering of the History Department, a monthly coffee klatsch, but by getting on this bus I'd acknowledged that it didn't matter any-more if I spent time among my colleagues or ended up dozens of miles away listening to jazz.

Our bus left the interstate and turned onto the Old Highway. My friend Vince across the aisle, who appeared to be in his early fifties, was telling me about a friend who'd been on his mind a lot recently. "He died two years ago. Three years ago, I think. He destroyed, just destroyed, his liver. He swelled up bigger than a fucking toad. That's the third guy I've seen do that. He swelled up this big around," and so on. I didn't mind very much. Vince had a colorful past, had been married often, worked at hazardous jobs, fought in the Vietnam war, spent 210 days in jail the previous year for assaulting an alcoholism counselor right in the counselor's office, and, like many people you sit beside on the bus, as I'd found out since I'd quit driving a car, he apparently ran through this history repeatedly in the privacy of his thoughts and felt proud to share it with any polite listener. Overhead, the sky continued clear. The fields had been plowed in straight rows, but nothing had sprouted yet, and from here to every horizon we saw only the fastidious organization of lifeless dirt. Come late August the horizon would no longer be visible. The Old Highway would drill like a tunnel through tall corn. The sound of insects in the fields would be deafening, and above it all would carry the call, the whir-and-twitter, of redwing blackbirds. Right now we drifted through a soft ocher haze of dust.

Here along the Sioux, I saw as the bus carried us into Riverside in a bubble of air-conditioned artificial silence, Sam Clemens would have truly felt at home. Here was a river town with a Tom Sawyer feel, sunny and muggy and lazy, whose silence continued after we'd stepped out into the heat, life in general so quiet the flies were audible.

The bus stopped before a tobacco-and-fireworks stand run by two women decked in turquoise and wearing buckskin gowns and beaded headbands. Nearby several longhaired Indian men stood around talking, in jeans and boots and checkered shirts with the tails hanging out. Two of them clutched at one another, empty-eyed and drunk, waltzing together with such languor it took a minute to understand they were fighting. The Old Highway kept on across the river and quickly out of town, intersecting the main street and the weedy swatch of railroad right-of-way paralleling it. There were two casinos, each with its nightclub and restaurant, one with a small motel. Otherwise the town seemed built of service stations, hardware stores, lumber yards.

Vince urged me to come to his favored casino, the one closer to the water. By this time I could see he'd attached himself to me, and I went along.

Near the river the air felt even wetter and heavier. There were budding willow trees, and somewhere loud cicadas. The waterfront smelled of agricultural chemicals but also of something sweet and strangely familiar, like cotton candy. Joined as it was to the Mississippi, the river reached a finger of the South into the region, while the casinos, one russet, one sky blue, both covered with murals depicting empty arid desert scenes, and Vince's with a tall eagle-topped Styrofoam totem pole, labored to produce a Western flavor.

Smokey Henderson's trio was in fact playing in town, and right here at Vince's gambling spot. According to the poster just inside the tavern's entrance, they didn't strike up until the evening. Of course I'd known this but hadn't consciously considered it. I hadn't asked about return buses, either. I think I really intended to stay overnight, drinking and gambling to the detriment of my health and finances. Excessively, in other words. I couldn't expect to find much to distract me until I started. Why should I? Why should anything be going on in the sunny lifeless afternoon, why would there be any attempt to entertain these retirees interested only in killing the most time with the least number of quarters? But apparently something was happening inside, past the barroom where Vince and I sat. A half-dozen young women had assembled in a clump at the back of the large room, and a couple more were just coming from the darker recesses, the entrance to a showroom with a stage. "You ain't getting me back there to watch little girls shake their pussies," Vince told the bartender, taking me by the arm and sitting me on a bar stool beside him. "Naked girls used to make me howl, but now they just give me a serious dose of heartache. Ask me what my favorite pastime is and I'll tell you: My favorite pastime is blackjack. I'm too fat and I'm too old."

Vince ordered vodka. I had a club soda. From the showroom came disco music with a booming bass and a crisp piercing treble. Apparently, I gathered as he and the bartender discussed it, an amateur striptease contest was in full swing. The several young women around the place may have been amateurs, but they looked like professional strippers on break in their silken dressing gowns, kissing their cigarettes so as not to endanger their lipstick, guiding their gestures so as to protect their long false nails.

The blipping of video gambling games underlay everything. To one side we had the entrance to the dance competition, and on our right the barroom gave way to an acre of space ranked with electronic slot machines. I saw no crap tables, no roulette, only these instruments sounding like young waterfowl. Vince assured me they kept three tables in the back where live blackjack was played.

As soon as we had our drinks in hand, Vince, talking over his shoulder the whole time, led me into the back room toward the dancing in which he'd claimed to have no interest. He stood well under six feet, but he had tremendous mass and solidity and moved like an ocean liner among the small tables. Just following his silhouette in the near-dark I had the impression that all of his life whatever he'd approached had given way, that if he chose to keep walking now he would explode, if very very slowly, right out through the opposite wall. He got to a vacant table and sat with his back to the stage, where a woman in a thong and nothing else shook her hips and raised her arms and wobbled her breasts. "Skin to win!" somebody shouted, and others took it up, but the loud canned accompaniment stopped abruptly and she danced offstage smiling and bowing.

During the next ten minutes two more women came out heavily clothed and got down pretty quickly to their bare chests and G-strings. Meanwhile Vince kept on in a voice not loud and clear but certainly audible. Lots of his acquaintances, he seemed to be saying, had an inexplicable natural knack for gambling. "Or my brother. Take him. The sonofabitch bastard is just plain dumb-lucky. What can I say? Some people. If he buys a lottery ticket, it's gonna hit. Not the big hit, but just enough to where, I mean, he'll come home with twenty tickets and a six-pack and scratch off enough of them ten-dollar jobbies to drink for the next week. Then he'll sit around stupid drunk on three beers and say such ridiculous stuff I just wanna drop the sonofabitch. I mean just slap him till his eyes bleed. I mean, the question has to be answered: How long can two guys, two grown-ups, live in one single trailer? It was Mom's, and she left it to him, at least that's the way the will was written, but it's mine just as equally, I think he understands that. Anyway, the point is," Vince said, "mankind was not bred for the close confines. You can get trained to it, but one day you might just shoot somebody. Oh sure, yeah, it works in the military, or in jail, but there they got you locked up, they got their finger on your spine."

I doubt there were more than a dozen others at the tables around us. All men. Middle-aged, middle-income, midwestern. Golfers. In this twilight they were more imagined than seen, but I felt surrounded by the practitioners of a sacred mediocrity, an elegant mediocrity cloistering inaccessible tortures. I don't know quite how to put it. People, men, proud of their clichés yet full of helpless poetry. Meanwhile the music whamming and bamming. The women shaking themselves almost shyly.

Vince spent a good half-minute lighting a cigarette while the MC came onstage behind him. This was a small Asian or Native American woman in a black pantsuit who introduced each dancer again—there had been nine total—and delivered the decision of the judges, who were nowhere to be seen, and summoned forward the winner, a woman in a black Cleopatra-style wig wearing red bikini bottoms and a red vest with quivering red fringe. She tiptoed barefoot onto the stage and received her prize money in a large envelope which the MC was obliged to stick in the waist of her briefs because she held a tall bottle of beer in one hand and a cigarette in the other. Her face was a beautified mask, like a Kabuki player's. They gave her name as "O. O'Malley," or close to that. But as a matter of actual fact, she was Flower Cannon.

"I know her!" I said to Vince.

"Who? Her?" he said, turning around briefly. "Yeah, she's here every other Friday. She wins about half the time."

The music started again but not quite so loud. The stage went dark. Flower Cannon stood bent over in the corner putting on a pair of tennis shoes. She straightened up and raised her beer to her mouth and guzzled. Now she wore an old overcoat like a chemist's smock.

"Show's over, time to play cards," Vince said. But Vince seemed much more interested in continuing his monologue than in getting to his favorite pastime. As he talked he worked his eyebrows nonstop; they arched and flattened calisthenically. He seemed to be signaling wildly from somewhere inside himself while he confided in a casual tone.

Suddenly I said, "She shaves her pussy."

His cigarette stopped just short of his lips. He looked at me, squinting past the smoke. "Yeah, a lot of them do that."

"She shaves her cunt bare," I said.

Vomiting up these cruel vulgarities forced the blood into my head. Please remember, I wasn't drunk, hadn't had a sip of anything stronger than club soda. I felt happy, there's no other way of putting it.

I said, "I know her. I'll probably fuck her one of these days."

Vince stayed quite still for a couple seconds more. "I doubt that," he said.

Vince got louder as he drank another round, and then another. I didn't know what he was saying. I listened while peering mainly at his eyebrows. Every now and then I answered. It was the kind of barroom conversation in which two people talk at cross-purposes until, sometimes anyway, one punches the other one.

My habit when I've been humiliated is to go out and buy a book. When I wiped out a small IRA by trading like a crazy roulette addict, I bought a book on stocks. When I played golf in the Virginia suburbs and everybody laughed, I found a book by Gary Player; after some practice I got pretty good, good enough to like these outings with lobbyists. After this incident in a bar I found a book in a small, exotic store: *101 Defenses Against Attack.* I see I'm stalling. My friend slugged me. His fist snaked out like the knotted end of a whip and struck my forehead and the bridge of my nose. A polar whiteness exploded in my face. And although I wasn't out, didn't sleep, my thoughts all turned to questions, and I tipped over onto the floor. Sat there trying to push myself upright. I'm sure everybody thought I was drunk.

Under my hands the floor felt gritty with what I thought might be sawdust. It took me a little more time to remember what I was doing down there—I was trying to get up. I looked up to see Flower Cannon beside the stage. She'd taken off her black wig. She had her drink tipped up high and she was looking at me sideways. But out of a sort of libertarian barroom tact, I think, neither she nor anybody else seemed to be making very much of this incident. A couple of guys from a neighboring table helped me back onto my chair while I said, "I'm all right, I'm all right."

Vince himself had disappeared, and a good thing—a person with his criminal history couldn't afford any more trouble.

As soon as I could stand up straight, I left. On my way out I suddenly felt dizzy and sat down at the bar and asked for some orange juice. I sipped at it no more than a couple of minutes and then made my way out to the bright parking lot, where I realized I hadn't even stopped off at the men's room to see to my condition. My hands were filthy where I'd pushed myself up from the floor. Along with the grit of sawdust I found the stains of spilt drinks on my knees where I'd crawled around looking for my senses. I began to realize I had no idea where in the world I was going.

A man approached me, a young man frowning intelligently. Apparently he'd followed me out of the casino. "I saw that in there," he said.

I leaned against a car.

"You okay?"

I nodded and tried to smile. "Excellent."

In retrospect, there's the humiliation: I forgot to be out-raged, tried to play the cowboy.

"If you want to press charges, I'll show up in court."

"It was just one of those ridiculous—aah," I assured him incoherently, "you know how it goes."

"That was a completely unprovoked attack."

I recognized him. He was a grad student with an office in our building, the Humanities Building. I didn't know what subject he taught, but whenever I went down the stairs I passed his office, and it seemed he was always there, always talking in a self-assured nonstop voice to one of his students while others waited outside his door or sat on the stairs nearby. In a way, he was a junior colleague of mine. My embarrassment was now complete.

"If there's anything I can do—"

"I'd really feel worse if you troubled yourself about it at all."

"Yeah, I get you," he said. "Okay."

"Thanks."

"Just tell me you're navigating on your own power, and I'm outa here."

"I just needed air. I'm all right."

After he'd left me I moved myself a few paces and sat on the bumper of a truck while I tried to make a plan for the rest of the day, which looked completely unappealing now. I determined I'd check on bus schedules. If I didn't learn of a bus leaving very soon, I'd get a motel room and watch TV or nap while I waited.

But now I found myself signaling across the parking lot to Flower Cannon as she came out of the casino. She headed right over, whether to greet me or because her car was parked close by I didn't know.

"Hi."

"Hi," she said. She was wearing jeans and a man's wrinkled linen sports coat. Her makeup was gone.

"We're actually acquainted," I said.

"Yes. Hi," she said.

"Do you remember me?"

"Sure. You just got knocked out in there. You're quite memorable."

"I was just going to ask you for a ride back to the University, if you remember me."

"Michael Reed, right?"

"Yes. Michael Reed. I need a ride."

"Did he steal your car, too?"

"I'm glad one of us sees the humor in it."

"Oh. I'm sorry," she said. "I'm just laughing because I'm drunk."

"Drunk? And you're driving?"

"All over the road like a goddamn maniac. We've got plenty of room," she said. "Hop right in."

Actually her grad-student Japanese hatchback was crowded with boxes, books, clothing, trash. I cleared a space on the passenger side by shoveling junk over the back of the seat.

"I'm sorry it smells funny," she said. "It needs to go through the car wash sometime with the windows open."

She started the car after a couple of tries. "Wasn't there somebody else?" I asked.

"Who?"

"I don't know. Who's we?"

"We?"

"You said we. Who's we?"

"I don't know. You and me."

"Okay. I just didn't want to forget someone."

"Who?"

"I don't know."

"Fuck 'em," she said, "whoever they are," and we swooped out of the lot.

I'd stayed in Riverside no more than two hours, probably less, been conveyed there swiftly and stayed briefly to be assaulted and now was conveyed back again over the flat landscape where the fields lay in perfect sterile rows of dust. I felt wonderful in a way. But my head ached.

"I missed your act," I told her. "What was the alias you performed under?"

"'O. O. O'Malley,'" she said.

"And you won."

"I sure did."

"Very good."

"You take it all off, you get the prize. Gynecology triumphs."

"I missed that."

"'Skin to win.'"

"Excellent." I couldn't really converse. I worried about

Flower's driving. She didn't give it her full attention. She took her eyes off the road whenever she addressed me and had a trick of jamming the gas suddenly and accelerating up into the seventies for no good reason. In a sports car she'd be a demon. I could feel the cogs and guys of the steering about to snap. I worried about the tires, certainly they were the cheapest. Yes, sometimes part of me wanted my life to end like this, in a bad wreck, as a way of sharing the horror of Anne and Elsie's last moments. But the rest of me was just inordinately afraid in a car.

Flower dropped me at the gate to the Humanities Building parking lot.

"Are you going in?" She shut the engine off and turned herself toward me.

"Going in. Yes. Why wouldn't I be going in?"

"I don't know. I thought maybe your car was parked here or something."

"I don't have a car. I'm going in."

What do I see when I remember her face? Those eyes. In fact they were mind-wrecking. Blue and pitiable and sweet, in their deep dark sockets, though I wish for some other word than sockets. When I looked into them my thoughts just stopped.

"Well, fix your face first. You're smudgy," she said. She had a funny way at the ends of her sentences. Rather than a pause, she created a plunge.

"How much was the prize for your dance?"

"One-fifty."

"That's not bad."

"It's two fifty on the Fourth of July."

"Maybe I should try to be there," I told her.

"Sure. I'll give you a lift," she said. "Since you don't have a car."

I went in through the basement entrance and checked my reflection in a mirror in the men's room. The wild punch had dented my forehead near the scalp. I didn't look like a brawler so much as a man who forgot to watch where he was going. I wet my hair and pasted a forelock over the red area and went upstairs to the monthly Department of History coffee klatsch. I was pretty much the last to arrive, and as I entered the small lounge, always to me somehow reminiscent of a prison's visiting area, they all looked up from their conversations. Then the dozen or so of them welcomed me almost as a reception line, one by one. As if I'd done something special I didn't know about.

This was curious, even slightly disorienting. I sipped coffee and ate a cookie until their attention drifted away from me and I was left dusting powdered sugar from my fingers.

Tiberius Soames greeted me with a sort of wise and happy weariness. He put his hand on my shoulder. "You've been worried about me. And I appreciate that. But no. I'm fine. Yes."

"You sound all right," I said. And we went together toward the pair of urns and drew ourselves more completely unnecessary coffee.

Soames seemed to discover the Styrofoam cup in his hand, gulped at it gratefully. "I've just got no more stomach for the bitter charade. When my mother died her body was eaten by dogs."

I tried to think of some words to say. I tried, but I couldn't. "Dogs?" was the best I could do.

"That's my message to the world. Why should it be otherwise? Should I disguise the facts concerning our universe?"

"Tiberius—" Many people called him Tibby, but I didn't know him that well, and anyway he might be going crazy right before our eyes. The situation seemed to call for full names.

This thought brought back the moment I'd had with the patient at the Swan's Grove campus, with his head trauma and his upraised invisible flame. It seemed just the kind of remark the patient might have made. When my mother died her body was eaten by dogs. Instead the man had given me his name and address and I still had them somewhere among my notes. Robert Hicks.

Tiberius said, "All right then. I'll stop alarming you and say something trivial and muy apropos. For instance, do you have any German? No. Okay then. You'll be interested to know that in German *klatsch* means 'gossip.' Here is our wonderful hostess; *sprechen zie Deutsch*?" he asked as Clara Frenow approached, whisking crumbs from her bosom and getting frosting on her neckline in the process. "At du klatsch we are torn by dogs."

"I think you said," she said, "did you say—?"

"Yes, in an attempt to be appropriately trivial and at the same time Germanic just somewhat. Clara. My goddess. Are you the originator of the idea that we should occasionally *klatsch* together?"

"Uh. Yes," she said. "Rather I mean—no, Tibby. It's been a

tradition since the seventies." Clara had completed her round of chemotherapy. She didn't wear a wig, but covered her patchy baldness with an assortment of caps, baseball caps, knit caps, hats of felt, of straw, a sailor's hat, today a jaunty blue beret that made her look like an English schoolgirl. For a few weeks her battle had shot her full of fire. She'd been running over with new ideas and seemed to be viewing the materials of her life from a mountaintop. The fight had apparently been successful, the cancer was driven back, and now Clara seemed her sad self again.

And weren't we all just as sad? These little gatherings where you can smell the sugar, the small cakes. Ours were come-as-you-are, but you couldn't make these occasions any more bearable by wearing shorts and tennis shoes. Stainless steel urns on brown institutional tables hidden under white paper lace. Professor Frenow in her pitifully jaunty headgear, Tiberius Soames with his fingertips at a floating braille, looking as if the air hurt his skin. He stayed near me but was silent. He smiled a wide terrified distracted smile. I couldn't tell if he was pained for me or for himself.

The History Department was thriving, thanks entirely to Soames. As a young diplomat in the Haitian government, I believe an assistant to the President's Chargé d'Affaires, he'd been implicated in a coup conspiracy, quite accurately, he said, and I didn't doubt him. He escaped to France and received political refugee status, which protected him from extradition. He claimed to have been spirited to Paris by the British MI-6. When he talked of his past he had a habit of stating somewhere invariably in the tale, "All the boys in MI-6 went to the same school and shared a horrible adolescence." This information meant something to him. He was always turning it over in his mind, apparently, but as far as I know he never got its significance across to any of the rest of us. The kids adored his personal reminiscences, stories that sometimes hijacked whole lecture periods but which he tied to the study of history in a way that illuminated it as the very medium of our lives. Here, after all, stood a man who lived under sentence of death in the land of his fathers. History had done that. He would never return. He'd written half a dozen books, contributed frequently to *Foreign Affairs,* and had a good exile. Still, it was exile.

Clara rang her spoon against her cup and delivered a toast. A toast to me. The purpose of today's gathering was to celebrate me. Because I was leaving. Everyone applauded politely.

Apparently they weren't going to renew my contract. This was news. I'd expected one more appointment, and then the gate. Clara and I had chatted at the end of the previous year and left the subject open; somehow it had closed all by itself. Here I'd been wondering what would happen to me year after next, and it was happening now.

I wondered if, in the shuffle of medicines and sorrows through her recent life, Clara had simply forgotten to discuss this with me. As I tumbled it all over in my mind, smiling and faking my thanks, bitter and relieved, I considered she'd probably at first simply hoped, and finally just presumed, that no discussion was necessary. Out of sheer personal cowardice she may have decided to let that one conversation serve as the final and necessary acknowledgement that, as far as History was concerned, I was history. But that was the style in our Department, and, as far as I knew, in all the other Departments. We conducted our business with a nonconfrontational vagueness which, in the world I'd been formerly a part of, the political realm, had been saved for communication with the voters (the Senator had called them "the votes"). To constituents we equivocated, but behind closed doors nobody minced words.

I heard a female campaign manager say to an aide once, "Do you want to know how a loser stinks? Put your nose in your armpit. Then empty your desk." Maybe in the academy a distaste for causing pain kept us from shafting one another quite so mercilessly, but I don't think Clara's way of firing someone was very much more adroit, and I doubt the young aide clearing out his desk drawers had felt any more astonished and red-faced that day than I did at the moment.

Suddenly Soames was lucid: "Are you secretly ready to get out of this place?"

"I can feel the whole experience withering around me."

"Perfect! You understand me perfectly. Do you remember the dead skins of the Pulitzer Prize winner? Right. His books— dead skins! How could he say that? Do you think he was being stupidly provocative or simply imitating a colossal human anus?"

"He treated me okay, Tiberius. But I wasn't chasing his girlfriend around the living room."

"Oh, my friends and foes! That night! Later! You have no idea how violently I masturbated!"

Let that be the last word of any description of the conversations among our Department members.

But no, I couldn't let it. A few minutes later I trailed Clara Frenow into the hallway and called her name as she struggled with her office door.

"I'm surprised I even feel irritated with you," I told her.

She looked surprised herself, then unsurprised, then incapable of surprise. "You want to come in?" she said.

It was visible and plain, the oppressiveness stealing back over her life. And all she had was her blue beret. She looked prehistoric. I could see her in the rags of animals, lifting up a small harpoon against the storm.

"Nah," I said, "forget it, no."

Tiberius hadn't had his last word, either. He turned up beside me now and put both hands on my arm: "Michael, we must get out of this flatness. The flatness and the regimented plant life. The vastly regimented plant life. Nothing matters but that we get out of here."

He walked away toward the hallway's end. He hadn't even glanced at Clara. In the stairwell he became a swaying silhouette and disappeared six inches at a time, descending.

"Clara, I thought we had an understanding." But I might as well have been saying, I understood we had a thought.

"Well, I don't know about that."

"Then I guess we didn't. It's probably silly of me to be talking about it. Anyway—come on. What happened?"

"The position's gone tenure track. It was kind of sudden, Mike."

We both knew I'd done nothing to build a case for getting tenure.

"We assumed it was coming, but it came without warning," she explained. "The fact is Marty blessed us suddenly with the tenured slot when Tiberius got all that publicity. Look, we've got to move Tiberius over to a tenure track. In fact we'd better give him tenure right away or we're going to lose him."

"If you haven't already."

"He's not as around-the-bend as he acts. He's just lighting a fire under us. And having fun at it, too, I might add."

Marty Peele was the Dean of Liberal Arts (and the man at whose house Tiberius had been so pleased to meet Kelly Stein). The History Department was barely on Marty's radar, but apparently he'd been galvanized by a series of interviews Tiberius had done with somebody on PBS. Soames had been brilliant. That which excellent teaching couldn't do for him, the impression that he'd become famous had managed to do. And good for him.

"Good for him. And, really: good for the Department. And good for the whole institution. It just comes kind of abruptly—as you say."

"I would have shuffled you over to Tibby's position for a year, but the truth is, we had to restructure the budget, too. In effect his line isn't there, not for a year or two anyway."

"You mean it isn't there at all?"

"Well, it's sort of there. There just isn't much money for

it." Tiberius had probably gotten a whopping raise, in other words.

"I could maybe do with that. Just for the one year."

"Well, of course, Mike. If you want the position—uh." She finished off by saying, nearly wailing, "Oh, Mike!"

"Oh, Clara!" It was impossible. I'd been wrong to ask. "All right. I feel like a fool. I know you've done whatever you could. I'm out of line. I owe you thanks, and that's all."

"You've been wonderful here," she said.

"It's been good for me." I was sincere in saying it.

I took the stairs to the parking-lot entrance. When I reached the street I didn't know whether to go right or left. Soon I'd have to start acting like a person who cared about what happened to him.

Not a lot happened. The following day I carried a cardboard box to the office and emptied my desk into it. Over the next two weeks I brought several such boxes into the house I rented. Slowly I packed, as yet without a destination. I watched the weather turn.

Just before the end of the academic year I took a trip to upstate New York to attend the Conference on Emerging Democracies. I flew by jet to New York City, and from there I rode a train. I had no preparations to make, no real role to play at the Conference, a gathering sponsored by the Giddings Policy Studies Foundation and an annual tradition since the days when "democracy" had meant "socialism," a roundup of intellectuals currently undertaking a project of cool-headed, not to say bald-faced, retrenchment. I spent a very long three-day weekend among a lot of people who, I was sort of glad to see, had no intention of abandoning their earliest and most hopeful assumptions. Sixteen weeks before, the Berlin Wall had come down. Nobody mentioned this. The term "Marxist" flew all around the place, but none of the speakers ever referred to The Left or The Revolution or The People. On panels, behind podiums—so tiny in nearly empty auditoriums—they displayed the vivid, liberated staunchness of spinsters in old novels. What they'd mistaken for a political philosophy had always amounted, they were seeing now, to an aesthetic, and the divorce it was undergoing from its previous claim to relevance could only serve to purify it. They were no-nonsense about being all nonsense. This didn't preclude a certain shift in personal style. The men no longer smoked pipes of tobacco, and the women no longer drank sherry or wore bright lipstick inexpertly applied. I don't know why I went. I think I wanted something to happen to me there but nothing did.

Except that I spent a couple of days in the city and was struck as always with how dirty and beautiful New York is. The gray light is a song. And the grafitti alongside the Amtrak: The rails head north out of Penn Station under the streets, almost as through a tunnel, alongside the passing logos of gangs and solitary hit-artists who use the patches of sunshine that fall into the brief spaces between overpasses, their fat names ballooning into the foreground of their strange works, switched on and off in alternating zones of light and dark. They make the letters of our own alphabet look like foreign ideograms, ignorant, rudely dismissive, also happy: magical bursting stars, spirals, lightning. And I realized that what I first require of a work of art is that its agenda—is that the word I want?—not include me. I don't want its aims put in doubt by an attempt to appeal to me, by any awareness of me at all.

What brought Flower Cannon to mind right then I don't know, but I have to say the passing parade put my recent experiences with her into a kind of persective. The experiences were mostly about seeing her, laying eyes on her—not about hearing her words, certainly not about touching her. And now I think this narrative might cohere, if I ask you to fix it with this vision: luminous images, summoned and dismissed in a flowing vagueness. The difference being that I didn't take Flower for a message, but a ghost, the ghost of my daughter—yes, and for a while she came and went in the flow of events like my Elsie in the silent cataract of memory.

The picture I've been giving here is that of the most circumscribed and uneventful period of my life. In the last few weeks, more had happened to me than I'd experienced in years—developing a small but impossible crush on a student, getting socked in the head, losing my job a year earlier than I'd expected, taking a pointless journey. I needed one more aberration in the round I'd been following, one more liberating aberration, before I broke gently free and continued on a new path. I'd say I was almost conscious of needing it. Almost consciously looking for trouble.

The final event on my calendar would be the expiration of my lease at the end of June. I should get out of town before then. I had no summer classes, no business here, no people keeping me—my time was up. But when classes ended in the spring, I didn't go.

By the middle of June the town seemed stunned by the summer, emptied of nearly half its people, after all, and the livelier half at that. It was hot. Humid. I was idle. Bored. Almost every weekday afternoon I met Ted MacKey at an air-conditioned basement tavern and watched him get drunk. Then we went to our separate dinners.

Sometimes Eloise Sprungl joined us. She was the woman who catered many of the dinners for the Liberal Arts faculty. I've described her as the image of Peter Lorre. For some years she'd been tenured faculty in the Art Department and had even done a turn as department chair, but one day she'd simply stopped showing up for work. Tendered her resignation. She painted almost daily now, had a studio in her home, but she didn't think she was any good. All this and more she told me in the time it took her to smoke a cigarette and down a double schnapps while we waited for Ted to come wobbling down the stairs of Dooley Noodle's, the basement tavern—the first moment she and I were ever alone together. She revealed that two years before, her husband had died of lymphoma, a complication of AIDS.

At one time or another she claimed to have bombed a power plant in the seventies, to have invented a process used in long-range observatory telescopes, and to have conducted, as a girl of thirteen, a red-hot love affair with Ernest Hemingway that spanned the globe, and she hinted she was the reason he'd ended it all. She liked referring to herself as the Froggy Bitch. "Give the Froggy Bitch a light . . ." "The Froggy Bitch must excuse herself to pee . . ." "Even the Froggy Bitch gets hungry, so let's eat!" Yet with all that had happened to her, she seemed neither sad nor angry. I'm not sure why I bother talking about Eloise except to reflect, for my own benefit, on the kind of people I was drawn to. State-run education was mostly show. She and Ted Mackey were open about that. They were just the type to thrive in these vapors of low-lying cynicism, occasional genius, and small polite terror.

And Ted has, in fact, continued to flourish. So has Eloise Sprungl. And although I see I'm not yet quite finished recording these memories, I might as well tell about some of the others:

Clara Frenow beat the cancer permanently, took early retirement, and either joined the Peace Corps or bought a bed-and-breakfast in Minnesota, so the reports went. Maybe she did both. As for Flower Cannon, I have no idea what's become of her, but if I ever track her down I'm sure she'll be up to something quite shocking and also absolutely no surprise. Of course all along I've been disingenuous when referring to Tiberius Soames, as I'm sure the name was familiar. Three years ago he and Marcel Delahey shared the Nobel Prize for economics. He's got a big endowed chair now at the University of Chicago and all day long does whatever he wants. Ted MacKey and I still correspond, or anyway exchange postcards.

His last: "I'm pimping a couple co-eds now, and I've joined a coven. Marie [his wife] has had a sex change. We never liked you. Keep in touch." The photo shows a vast field of profoundly green cultivated rows across which he's scrawled *excuse the corny sentiment.*

And, of prizes: You may be aware of T. K. Nickerson's Pulitzer—his second Pulitzer—the year before last. I bought the book, found it unreadable. He followed quickly with another, which I picked up browsing in a store one day and which by that evening I'd devoured in one sitting, and I've since read it again with just as much pleasure. So he still knows how to write. He married Kelly Stein, or so I think I heard. And what about J.J.? Two years back this short letter came to me, and I haven't yet tossed it out:

Dear Michael,

This is going to be a strange little note, Mike, but I can't shake this annoying ridiculous sense I have that I said something I didn't finish, but have to get said completely. It's selfish of me to bother you with this, because you're no more involved than in the capacity of the chance bystander, poor guy. But I'm not explaining, so I'll explain. After the night I had dinner with you at Capiche, the night I learned of Trevor Watt's passing, I told you he'd been important at first and then I realized I hadn't thought of him in years. The uncompleted thought is this: No, that was wrong, and I should have gone on to say: Now he's dead and I realize I feel free, because whether he's occupied my thoughts or not, Trevor has always been there. Always riding me, riding my life. As melodramatic as that sounds. And now he's dead and the weight is lifted. What a happy death! That's what I want to say, and do you see I couldn't say it to anyone who actually knew him. I suppose you do see that. So you get the news: What a happy, wonderful death!"

J.J. goes on to say he's seen a piece of mine in *Men's Journal*. "What a coup!" he says. I don't hold the sarcasm against him.

Otherwise I've had nothing from any of that bunch, except, as I've said, the occasional card from Ted MacKey, whom I invite you to imagine facing me in a booth those several years ago in a basement tavern, our hands around cold drinks, while outside the Midwest pounded in a heat wave. Eloise was with us too. She didn't talk much today. Ted leaned toward me, drunk, huddled around some inner upright and saying only, "You don't know. You don't. You just don't know." He'd fed some dollars to the jukebox and set it to play "Let Me Roll It" by Paul McCartney infinitely. After a few drinks Ted conversed very little. He mostly sang.

I went down to St. James Infirmary
And I saw my baby there.
She was stretched out on a long white table,
So still, so cold, so bare,

he was singing now (while the jukebox played Paul McCartney).

Let her go, let her go, God bless her,

he sang, throwing wide his arms.

Wherever she may be. . . .

By wrecking the rhythm, he braided the old spiritual together with the McCartney tune coming out of the jukebox, and made an odd duet.

"Reed," he said, "Reed. Just, man—bury me where the corn don't grow."

Eloise laughed and hacked. She had the smashed sinuses of an English bulldog.

Here I've let my memory veer down the stairs and float alongside the bar and hover in the light of the jukebox, when actually there's no point. Nothing worth telling about happened down there. Or up in the world, for that matter. I'd packed my few belongings in boxes and was ready to move to a motel until I found a reason to depart—until I had a destination. Other than that, the whole month of June had barely managed to occur. But it went out with a lot of noise.

On the twenty-ninth I drove Ted home from Dooley's because he seemed to think that was best. He hadn't thought so any of the other days he'd lurched to his feet after several drinks, announced he was hungry, and marched with a mechanical determination up the stairs. But today I drove him, and Eloise Sprungl, too. Ted insisted we go to his house first, however, because he wanted to show me something.

"Okay, what is it?" I asked when we'd pulled up in front of his big home.

"The car. I'm showing you the car."

"Well, it's an excellent car, Ted."

I hadn't driven a car in a long time, not in four years, plus three months. I liked driving the car.

"It's a 1985 BMW three-oh-two or two-oh-three, or—do you want it?"

"Want it. To own?"

"It's for sale."

"What's the price of one of these things?"

"Drive it."

"I just did."

"Drive it, man. Keep it a couple days. Let's talk. It's for sale and I want you to have it and it's for sale."

Ted's home was made of red brick. It had a small entry with white pillars, and a semicircle drive, also small, but there they were, the entry and the drive, saying, "This wants to be a mansion." To the side stood Ted's blond ten-year-old son in a white T-shirt and white shorts, puffing flagrantly with large gestures on a cigarette that wasn't actually burning. The player of the lute. Ted got out scolding and laughing. He grabbed his son's cigarette and tossed it aside and it bounced on the tight green crew cut of the lawn. Together they went into the house.

I held the steering wheel and tromped the accelerator of my new car. The decision was made as soon as the suggestion. I put off admitting it to Ted or even to myself, but the car was mine.

I took Eloise to her place across town. On the way I asked her if she'd been getting a lot of painting done, and she told me not much. "The catering's slack, and then I paint less. For some reason I work harder when I'm working harder. I'm practically on vacation. I couldn't keep up with any business anyhow. There's nobody experienced around to help me but Phil and Flower."

"That would be Flower Cannon maybe."

"Yes. She's—you know her. Have you had her?"

"Hey. Eloise."

"As a student, Mike."

"We're acquainted. I don't think she's interested in history."

"No, I wouldn't think so. This summer she's the mad cellist. They're getting together some kind of chamber group, I don't know. This is my place. What do you think of this contraption?" She meant the car.

"It's fine. I haven't driven in years. Anything's going to feel funny."

"A BMW can't feel *that* funny. How many miles? Ah, plenty." She was leaning over and peering at the odometer.

"If I don't wreck it by tomorrow, I guess I'll buy it."

"Buy it now! The asshole's drunk!" She kissed my cheek and got out.

"Do you run into Flower much, or not?" I asked her out the window.

"Flower? No." She both squinted and leered now. She had a limber face! "Are you after her?"

"After her? Wow. You're frank as hell, aren't you?"

"Usually I'd warn a young girl away from the prof. But in this case it's you who'd better take warning, pal." She leaned down and spoke with burnt tobacco and peppermint schnapps on her breath. "I *am* your pal, you know. In the end it's the likes of us who'll be stuck with each other." She stood up and addressed the population generally: "You'll end up marrying me, the Froggy Bitch with too many cats and a drinking problem every summer! And you'll thank God!

"At least you'll have a ritzy car!" she called after me as I drove away.

I had a vivid and disturbing dream that night that sent me out of my bed and down to the kitchen in my bathrobe to putter distractedly there until dawn. I think to recount your dreams is to bore the entire world, and I don't normally even trouble myself to recollect mine. But since it's developed, I think we can agree, that the knots in this line, the handholds, are those moments having to do with Flower Cannon, I'll tell about this one. I'm following Flower Cannon through bureaucratic hallways—the sort of place you find yourself in from time to time with a form in your hand, looking for an office where someone will take this thing and make sense of it, but I had no document, I had only this vague feminine figure somewhere ahead of me as a reason for my wandering. She disappeared in her white garb through a door halfway along a corridor. I now understood that this was a hospital, understood without having wondered, in the state of senility common to the dreaming mind. I followed her through the same door and walked out onto a glaring stage before a vast, shadowy audience of students. My quarry—yes? or my grail?—lay naked on a gurney while a doctor pointed his finger at her breasts and vagina and lectured unintelligibly. I didn't belong here. My shame was like a child's. I woke up sweating and chilled with panic. Instantly the words Ted MacKey had sung that afternoon came back:

> *I went down to St. James Infirmary*
> *And I saw my baby there.*
> *She was stretched out on a long white table,*
> *So still, so cold, so bare.*

As I've said, dreams are nonsense. But this one was a lot like something that actually happened the very next day. Around four that afternoon I was at the supermarket picking up a few items I probably didn't need urgently. (I like wandering the aisles and coming up with a couple of days' menu, just improvising. Then I let the stuff rot at home while I have myself fed in restaurants.) I was standing in the checkout lane reading the headlines of *Midnight* and *Globe* and the *National Enquirer,* trying not to take to heart the messages of the tabloid press: The mighty are fallen; glamor equals misery; the innocent shall be raped and killed. And then I saw Flower Cannon, hunched and straight-armed, shoving along a shopping cart.

She was all dressed up in a black-and-white pantsuit with pads that gave her sharp shoulders. Ankle-high white booties on her feet. The first strong impression was that of a crew member in a science-fiction tale. I waited just outside the store, hoping to say hi, but she came out the other exit. I trailed her through the parking lot and called her name, but she didn't acknowledge this man in a baking blacktop car park, brown paper bag of groceries dangling at his side in a single-handed grip, shouting, "Flower! Flower!"

I stood watching while she got aboard her hatchback, and then I went to my new used German and followed her. I was living last night's dream, only in a setting not of hallways but of shimmering black streets.

Flower wasn't going fast. I could have pulled alongside and signaled, but I didn't. We went about a mile out the Old Highway and then left onto a narrow concrete road that shot west with never a turning through fields of alfalfa, fields of barley, fields of knee-high rows of corn.

I kept the windows down. The world was mute and pungent, brilliantly green. A few miles along Flower turned left again into the gravel lot of a gray one-storey building and parked among a lot of other cars gathered together in the midst of this flat vastness. Nothing else to see but a distant pair of concrete grain elevators standing above the horizon. Every small sound came up crisp and then the breeze took it far away, the small steady wind across the crust of the world, the click of her door and her heels and toes on the gravel. Flower glanced my way without curiosity as she headed into the place.

It was a cheap structure almost on the order of a mobile home, but much larger inside than it had seemed. A wide hallway went either way out of a foyer where scores of people stood around without having to crowd. A sense of offices, meeting rooms, classrooms down institutional corridors. Directly ahead, double doors opened onto a chamber big enough, from what I could see, to accommodate hundreds. I thought I glimpsed church pews. Folks were wandering inside there to sit. I spotted Flower easily among all the farmers and the farmers' wives. She stood by the double doors in her black-and-white pantsuit, maybe a bit harlequinesque but very stylish and expensive looking, talking in sign language with a young boy about sixteen. He must have been a deaf boy. I was fascinated. Without voices to help them they used whatever they had, both their faces animated, exploding with emotion, while the quick lively gestures shot down their arms and out their fingers; they worked at it like silent-film actors. And suddenly, reminded of the old silent films, I was struck with an understanding of the empty peace the boy inhabited. He had a thin, elegant face, blond hair, blue eyes, clear complexion. None of the erupting skin or awkwardness of adolescence.

The people seemed friendly. Wherever I looked I got a nod and a smile. In a minute I was approached by two men. One told me I was welcome. The other said they'd just begun their summer schedule here. Therefore, the first told me, this wasn't Bible Study, as I'd probably expected.

I didn't bother telling them I'd expected nothing, or anything but this: I'd stumbled into Sing Night. They were some sort of religious fellowship, and this building was their church. One of my hosts led me into the large room, which was filled with many dozens of rustic wooden pews and fronted by a podium. We stood in the back while my companion, a man as small as I but more solid, in jeans and a long-sleeved white shirt, surveyed the place. One wide center aisle cut the room in half. The rows were filling up, women in the left-hand section, men in the right.

My host addressed me as a needy spirit, a groping soul. "We aren't about doctrine so much. We *do* have a pamphlet, but we aren't about doctrine, like I say. Did you get a—" The other man reappeared and handed me their pamphlet. "Here," my friend said. "You'll see in the first part right here where it says the important thing is—well, just take a look. The important thing is a—" He couldn't get himself to say it. It made it seem all the more important, whatever it was.

We three sat down together on the men's side of the room. I recognized that the crowd around me was one of those Protestant sects descended from Rhineland Anabaptists, like the Mennonites or the Amish. I might have seen any of them in town and never noticed, but in this large group it was plain they kept to a mode of dress. The women all wore skirts or dresses, rather long ones, and flat-heeled shoes and socks, and they kept their long hair in thick braids or pinned up. All of the men wore mustaches or beards. They'd picked me out right away, my face scraped bare, arms naked in my short sleeves, while theirs, both the women's and men's, buttoned at the wrists.

Very soon the rows were almost full. The voices quieted. We sat still, all facing forward. Nobody said a word. I heard no coughing, no clearing of throats. Birdsong, very faint, carried in from the fields. For five minutes or even longer the wooden podium at the front of the room stood solitary, and we watched it.

Then a man, just a voice from the crowd, suggested, "Let us pray."

The assembly couldn't have hit the floor quicker if someone had opened up in their midst with a machine gun. With one motion, all leapt down onto their knees facing backward, elbows on the pews. I acted as decisively as they, yanked by a human gravity, blown off my tail to cower with my elbows on the seat and my forehead against my knuckles, shocked out of my wits.

Somebody said a prayer, but I heard none of it.

Then, as if nothing had happened, as if the multitude had never suffered this astonishing collapse, we climbed back onto our seats. Again we had silence.

After a while a man's voice said, "Brother Fred, why don't you pick out a hymn?" I have no idea how this voice's owner, whom I couldn't see, was suddenly given the confidence to speak up, or what made him choose Brother Fred to lead us.

A young man stood, struggled down along the pew past a series of knees, and went quickly up the aisle to open a hymnal on the podium. He looked like all the others, with long sideburns, almost sidelocks, and a mustache and a white shirt. Around me everybody was taking hymnals from slots in the pew-backs. "Number two thirty-eight?" he said. "How about two thirty-eight?" The cover of the one I took up bore only the name *Friesland*. I found the hymn—

Sweet hour of prayer, sweet hour of prayer,
That calls me from a world of care
And bids me at my Father's throne
Make all my wants and wishes known.
In seasons of distress and grief,
My soul has often found relief
And oft escaped the Tempter's snare,
By thy return, sweet hour of prayer.

Their song astonished even more than their praying. They sang in multiple harmony, in a fullness and with a competence that didn't seem studied, but perfectly natural, innate, all talent. I heard none of the usual bad voices, none of the people you want to go up to and ask, "Could you please not sing?"

I kept my eye on Flower Cannon. She sat in the middle of the women, as I in the middle of the men. I wished I'd sat close enough to distinguish her voice, and let me go stronger and admit that I painfully regretted not hearing her sing. She looked very different from the others around her. They wore skirts and she wore slacks. No other woman had her head uncovered, none let her hair fall free or bared her arms. Flower's long red hair flowed down her back. Her blouse was sleeveless and her armpits stained with wide blotches of sweat. I made a note to myself—I had to get to a chemist someday, and ask if sweat is the same substance as tears.

The blond boy she'd been talking to sat two rows ahead of me. Once again it occurred to me—it more than occurred, the insight knocked the breath out of me—that the boy lived in a silence. Why on earth had he come? He sat quite still, completely self-possessed and perfectly alienated. For all he heard, he might have been in this chapel alone at midnight. Perhaps he was sensitive, in some tactile way, to an atmosphere thickened by hundreds of blended voices—how many? As the hymn swayed around me like wheat in a wind I found myself counting the house. Fourteen rows, about a dozen folks on each side of the aisle: nearly three hundred people, all singing beautifully. I wondered what it must sound like out in the empty green fields under the cloudless blue sky, how heartrendingly small even such a crowd of voices must sound rising up into the infinite indifference of outer space. I felt lonely for us all, and abruptly I knew there was no God.

I didn't think often about that which people called God, but for some time now I'd certainly hated it, this killer, this perpetrator, in whose blank silver eyes nobody was too insignificant, too unremarkable, too innocent and small to be overlooked in the parceling out of tragedy. I'd felt this all-powerful thing as a darkness and weight. Now it had vanished. A tight winding of chains had burst. Someone had unstuck my eyes. A huge ringing in my head had stopped. This is what the grand and lovely multitude of singers did to me.

I'm one of those who believes he can carry a tune, and so I sang, too, and nobody stopped me. Until just past six, for exactly an hour by my watch, we praised the empty universe. I felt our hearts going up and up into an endless interval with nothing to get in the way. All my happy liberated soul came out my throat.

Outside after the singing I stood talking with my self-appointed host, who explained that the sect was called the Friesland Fellowship, after its birthplace in the north of Holland, if I got it right. While he explained they didn't believe in insurance companies, military service, or state-supported education, I looked around for Flower.

She found us first. Apparently she'd noticed me earlier. She said hello and introduced her young companion.

"This is also Mike. Mike Reed, this is Mike Applegate. Mike has a date tonight."

"Which Mike?"

"Both Mikes. I'm loaning Mike Applegate my car. And Mike Reed could give me a lift to my studio. I could cook you up a little soup."

I told her I had a bag of groceries and a BMW, and she said that was perfect. All of this she repeated in mime and sign for the younger Mike. Remarkable how the expressions lit up her features and communicated the light to his. The evening's prospects were brilliant in his face. He held out his palm and she pointed toward her car and said, "The keys are in it." He understood.

We watched as the young blond Michael got into her hatchback with an angular ease, puffed out two short signals of exhaust, and took off fast.

"Well, this is slick," she said as we got to my car. "Is it fast?"

"Not as fast as you want it to be."

"Come on! These guys are built for the Autobahn."

"I know, but I'm not. I drive under the limit. It handles well," I said, feeling somehow required to offer a defense.

I took the Friesland Fellowship's pamphlet from my breast pocket and laid it on the dash while I started the car. Flower picked it up and looked at it, but all she said was, "Do you know what it sounds like, Michael? Like a mechanical animal."

And truly, the engine had a strongly mechanical yet somehow vocal sound when it accelerated. We entered the queue of vehicles heading onto the highway. The Frieslanders' will to conform seemed to reach deep into their choice of cars: minivans, well-equipped pickups, very few sedans, all of them in darker colors, and all fairly new.

"Where did you say we're going?"

"To my studio."

"Back in town?"

"No. Here. About two miles from here."

"Way out here in the country?"

"It's in the Tyson School. I'm living there."

Tyson was a town, or a village, I wasn't sure what it was.

All of this while I felt lifted by a strange new medium, a strange element—I now tell you that I was newly buoyant in a brighter life. In the midst of a hymn, God had disappeared. It was like waking from a nightmare in which I'd been paralyzed. Like discovering that gravity itself had been only a bad dream.

And here beside me was Flower Cannon dressed like an Andromedan cadet in her black-and-white zoot suit. I said, "Flower, explain yourself. Are you a prospect? What were you doing there?"

"I was there," and she hesitated . . . "for the music."

"Where did you meet him? Mike."

"Mike? The other Mike?"

"Mike Applegate."

"In signing class."

"I'm sorry?"

"Mike Applegate."

"I mean—"

"I met him in signing class. He was the teacher."

"I almost thought you said 'singing class.'"

She paused . . . "I don't guess he sings."

In her voice I heard that timbre, that attractive and dangerous timbre—as if an outburst of laughter were caught in her throat and making a sort of chamber of hilarity there.

"It was a twelve-hour class, two hours a night for six nights. It went fast, and we learned fast because our teacher couldn't talk out loud. And so I—and the others too, all of us who took the class—I sign differently from most hearing folks."

"How so?"

"They talk when they sign. I'm mute."

"I'm glad you're talking now."

She made great conversation, and entirely apart from its content. Her pauses were like pools. You wanted to draw closer until you were immersed. Some wealth of facial animation lingered from her previous discourse with the deaf Michael. I could hardly take my eyes away to look ahead, but it didn't matter. The road was ruthless, never bending.

"Was he just there for the car?"

Pause.

"He was there for the music."

We traveled slowly, washed along in an ocean of chlorophyll. Nothing existed out this way but tiny communities, widely spaced, each gathered around two or three monumental grain elevators. I didn't know the name of any of these towns, not that I supposed it mattered, and we didn't even reach the first, which must have been Tyson.

I told her, "I admire you."

She took a breath to speak but seemed to change her mind. Then said, "Why?"

"Because you do crazy things without having to be crazy."

"If you think I'm not crazy," she said, "you're out of your mind."

"I remember a comment you made once—and I thought you were looking right at me when you said it, is why I remember it so clearly. You said, 'Sane? Or tame?' Okay, but that's not the issue. The reason most of us seem so sane is we're clinging by our fingernails. But not you."

"And not you, either."

"Most everybody, I'd say."

"Not you. Not clinging. You're tied. You're tied to the mast, like Ulysses."

"I sure was."

"But not no more."

"No."

"Show me not no more, Michael Reed."

"You. Are you a siren? A witch?"

With a certain frustration I knew I spoke too soon, too urgently. I wanted to get out of the way the things I knew to say, wanted to say, the things I'd been thinking, all in the hope of moving into the unforeseen. The wind thundered around the car.

She said, "I'm a girl."

And now we arrived. I stopped the engine. The silence released our voices. But we had nothing further to say for the moment.

She'd directed us to a schoolhouse of orange brick in the midst of endless cultivated fields. The old building looked gigantic. Anything higher than a stalk of corn was visible for miles. A scraggly tree way off in the distance had the decisiveness of one clear fact.

We went up the steps. Flower used a key to the big front doors. How many times had I let myself into a silent public school after hours, to smell the lunches spoiling in lockers and the janitor's pungent wax, in the buildings of concrete and metal, exactly like our public prisons? This one was actually smaller than most, only four classrooms and an office on the first floor, and perfumed within by citrus and oil paint.

We took a short flight of steps into the basement and Flower put her key away again. For a purse she carried a small leather pouch that puckered with a string. She propped open the door at the far end of the hall, and the last of the day filled that region like a mist. The building felt irresistibly empty.

"Isn't it quiet?"

"It makes me want to run around breaking stuff."

"This is a public school building," she said. "I guess you could bust the windows, but everything else is indestructible."

In her basement studio, formerly a classroom, I sat on an institutional wooden chair, first putting down a handkerchief because the seat was daubed with paint. Everything was like that, every surface. I set down my plastic bag of produce on the floor next to her telephone, which was basically black but fingerprinted in a multitude of colors. Enough light came through ground-level windows—windows at the level of our heads. I watched her, not taking much in. Around the place I noticed three or four canvases on easels, all turned to the walls, the paintings hidden.

"Well! What do you think?"

"It's messy and full of ghosts," I said.

"The school's gone."

"I got that."

"They all go to a consolidated over in Hereford now. You can apply for space here through the state Arts Council."

"And are you allowed to live here?"

"No." She hadn't really entered, standing just inside the

door. She turned on the overhead fluorescents. "It's just a regulation," she said. "Nobody checks."

I told her I wasn't hungry but she said she was. I gave her my bag of groceries and waited alone, not moving a muscle, awkward and inexplicably ashamed, almost tearful with a sense of unbelonging, while she went to the janitor's closet down the hall to fill a saucepan with water. On a hotplate stashed randomly among a lot of junk on the wall-length counter she started things cooking. She handed me a knife and I stood up to help. I tried to wipe the paint from the blade but it was dry. I diced a carrot. The vertigo, the plunging shyness, passed. I cut up a cucumber. I asked what we were making and she said it was miso soup. I sliced an onion. "I'm crying," I said. "I'm crying, too," she said. "It's a good one."

Apparently Flower knew a bit of my history, the lousy part. "Do you cry a lot? Your family was wiped out, weren't they? So do you cry?"

"I used to but I stopped." We leaned against the counter as against a bar in a tavern, facing one another. "I think you remind me of my wife," I told her. "And I think you remind me of my daughter." As long as we were being blunt. "She was only twenty-three when we went to Washington."

"Not your daughter."

"My wife. Anne."

"Was she a whole lot younger than you?"

"About fourteen years. I was forty-four when she had our daughter, and I turned forty-nine three weeks after I lost them, the two of them. After they died."

"How old when they died?"

"Huntley was almost five. Anne was thirty-four."

"And now you are—"

"I'm fifty-three."

"And I'm twenty-six."

"You're young enough," I admitted, "that it's sort of the main thing about you."

"I'm less than half your age."

"Yeah. Finally. And next year you'll be more than half."

"You're getting younger and younger."

"When I'm two hundred? You'll be seven-eighths of the way there."

This silliness was all about nothing. I was enchanted with how easily it came.

She said, "It's funny the way mathematics works, Michael Reed."

She still had a strange ending to every statement. On my name her voice went over into the depths, and I went right along with it. Now she said, and I was sure she meant to flirt with me, "Let's just let that simmer right there."

She picked up a lab coat bunched on the counter, stepped behind a large blank canvas on an easel, and dropped her pants around her small black boots.

I sat on my chair again and watched. She stood backed by a white wall. The white canvas blocked all of her between her shoulders and knees. She managed to get out of her slacks without taking off her boots. She removed her blouse and hung it on the easel. Then she put on her gray smock.

We sat down at a collapsible table and moved aside her cluttered paints and pencils and ate our soup. Afterward I walked around. Against one wall I found her bed, just a pallet on the floor with a square pillow of dark silk, shot silk, I think it's called. All of her paintings faced the wall.

"Can I see what you're working on?"

"I don't think so. No. They aren't going anywhere."

"Why not?"

"I lack talent."

I wanted to lie with her on that pallet. To be very tired and sleep beside her all night.

Gradually the things she surrounded herself with, the materials she collected, were separating themselves from one another. I would live here among her bits of glass and shards of mirrors, strips and patches of astronomical and topographical maps, nautical charts; I'd live here in sunken Atlantis. It got bad light for a studio, all from the North and West, with the windows, though high in the room, set low to the ground outside. Or I would put her in the finest studio on earth.

She kept glass jars of buttons and boxes of marbles. Here was the lid of a large box like a tray holding multicolored strings and yarns, the silvery papery bark of a birch tree, small chrome and plastic emblems, the ones I could see saying *Satellite, Coconut, Rolls-a-Lot, Susie, Ramon, Camaro.* I was ready to fall in love. I was willing if she'd let me. On the floor against the wall among her leaning paintings was a black boom-box fingerprinted with the entire spectrum. It played low music, apparently always on. I thought I recognized an old Billy Srayhorn tune called "Blood Count."

I liked her environment very much. These intricate and unintelligible objects. Again I felt tremendously shy. I couldn't quite develop any of my reactions into a word.

Something was missing. She saw me looking around. "What?"

"Where's your big old cello?"

She laughed. "It's in the music building. I'm in a chamber group."

"Right. I heard."

"I'm pretty bad at that, too. But you can play just about any piece if you practice it enough."

"I think as long as we're getting a little personal," I said, "I'd better get right to the question on everybody's mind. What's your middle name?"

"No Middle Name," she said. "That's 'N.M.N.' on all the forms, but my sisters called me M 'n' M."

"Sisters! There are more of you? What a world."

"Two sisters. One's married to an out-of-work pseudo-actor-type asshole and the other has her own business, one of those catering trucks that sells lunch at construction sites. You know the ones with the shiny dimpled aluminum all over? The beautiful ones?"

"What are their names?—your sisters'—including middle names. If any."

"Daisy and Kali. After my maternal granny and the Hindu

goddess. So we just call her Goddess. As far as middle names, you'd better ask them. I don't think they'd like me to tell."

"The goddess of death?"

"You mean Kali?"

"Isn't Kali the goddess of death?"

"The goddess of death, yes, the blue one, with how many arms and those thick black eyebrows they all have, all those gods and goddesses."

"Wow."

"She looked good on a poster in a head shop. She looked quite beautiful and blue and they didn't know what she was the goddess of, with all her extra arms. They were new and hip, and they'd renounced all concepts. They were too hip to know anything at all."

"Your parents were flower children, maybe."

"No maybe! We all went to the Rainbow gatherings every summer. Every July Fourth until '93, for an orgy of pantheism and anarchy. After Goddess left home they moved to The Land—that huge commune down in Tennessee. My dad met Mom in '68 when he was a fisherman in Alaska. She worked every summer in Anchorage."

"Anchorage? Doing what?"

"Well. As a matter of fact she was a whore."

"Fantastic," was about all I could say.

"She made enough in ten weeks to live all year. I mean— back then. Before they met."

"Ten weeks..." She had a way of making anything I

could say sound stupid far in advance of my saying it.

"After they met, no, she quit the seasonal whoring, and then all she had was her memories."

"Of course, you could be kidding me."

That seemed to hurt her. "Why do you say that?"

Now we had one of those pauses, but it wasn't hers, it was mine, because I hadn't thought she could be wounded.

". . . I guess because I don't want to seem gullible."

"Okay. Nobody does. Should I tell you what I like about you?"

"That depends."

"I know. But I like you because you're small. Everything about you is the right size. Your spirit, too. Everything's portable. You're very self-contained. What do you like about me?"

Though I'd already said it once, it happened to be true, and so I said, "I admire you because you're wild."

She laughed at me for that.

I said, "Oh, you're wild. You're light. Even when you're perfectly still you're ready to be blown all around by the elements."

Now she looked shocked. "You did a pretty good job of stammering up till now. But that sounds rehearsed. Either that's a line of yours, or you've been thinking about me. Thinking actual words about me in your head."

"I dreamed about you last night."

"Tell me."

"No."

"Have you had fantasies about me?"

To get back something of myself, I crossed my arms over my chest. Ten feet away the radio still played jazz. She was still standing. I was still sitting in a chair. I felt like a pupil, a slow one. "You're a force on the planet, that's for sure. Where did you get that far-out name?"

"Have you imagined me? Am I your fantasy?"

"All right, yeah. You certainly are."

"And what have you fantasized, Michael Reed?"

"I don't know. This conversation is getting pretty close to it."

"Let me guess what you're thinking . . . Okay . . . And the answer is no."

"No?"

"No, they're not redheads."

"Who?"

"My sisters. They're brunettes."

"That's not what I was thinking."

"But Goddess bleaches hers out platinum. She's very L.A. All right—what were you really thinking?"

"I couldn't possibly remember now."

"I knew I could make you stop!"

"Okay, okay. I was thinking about your Fourth of July striptease competition. It's only five days away."

"Would you like to help me shave?"

"Shave?" That stopped my mouth for two long seconds. "Isn't it a little early for that?" Although inside I said only, Sweet gah-dam Jesus.

"Come and sit outside."

And I rose and followed her down the brief corridor, out the back door into the Midwest. She brought with her a small box of light wood—redwood, or cedar—built like a cigar box but naked of any design. When she saw me puzzling over it she opened the lid to show me it held a variety of envelopes, used envelopes, of many different sizes and colors, but generally of the sort for letters or greeting cards. We sat beside each other on the new grass, she with the box in her lap; and she fingered through the envelopes as if searching for one in particular. Her knee lay lightly against my hip. All this was fine, but it wasn't enough. I wanted something more than mere physical touch. Something unexpected. Something impossible to foresee. I looked at my watch: just past seven, the sun hanging and swelling, the shadows long and cool, though the heat still clung to the land. A banana moon stood above the horizon. Some clouds way to the north; they might disappear or they might bring hail and tornadoes. After these four years in the Midwest I'd learned to expect any kind of weather at any moment. I had rejected the weather, in a way, had walled myself off from any approach of the elements, had made them my enemy after the weather had become, in effect, the murderer of my wife and daughter.

Flower said, "Will you give me a sample of your handwriting?"

I didn't know how to respond to this. "I'm not sure."

"Write down a few words for me. A sentence, a phrase, a name, anything." She closed the box and set it in my lap. "Do you have a business card?"

Here I felt our movement toward the unforeseen, in the direction of something that couldn't have been predicted. I don't think I'll try to explain what I mean by that. Instead I'll hope it comes clear on its own. I put one of my business cards flat on the lid of the box and pushed the ball point from the pen with my thumb. A phrase? A name? I wrote: the name of the world—across the back of my card and set the box in Flower's lap.

She looked at my writing and read the phrase aloud. She opened the lid and put the card in one of the envelopes and closed it up with all the others inside their box and held it in her lap again. Her smock was buttoned high, came up just below the cleft of her neck and breastbone. There in her pale skin were one or two unbearably thin blue veins.

Why she wanted to spend this time with me I could only guess, because I was afraid to ask. I sat beside her looking at the daylit moon, wanting to kiss her, but afraid to. Also I had a powerful urge to leave, to get away from her, or from myself in this situation, but that idea scared me, too, because I saw myself five minutes down the road, braking and considering, accelerating and stopping, maybe even turning the car around in the big fields, the only person in the only car from horizon to horizon, and then turning the car around yet once again and heading home, wanting to go back to her, but afraid to.

Now I'm going to interrupt myself, and I don't know how to signal that except by saying it.

Looking over the pages of this reminiscence, I see I've misled. I've created the impression that what I've been aiming at is the account of a one-night stand, and that the item pending most crucially between Flower and me was my loss of a kind of late-life virginity. I've implied I'd had nothing to do with women since I'd lost my wife. That's not true.

The worst of my disequilibrium had passed in a couple of years. I wouldn't bore even a highly paid psychiatrist with the details of my love life, my sex life, during this period, except to say that it was quite a lot less than nothing—that is, I couldn't bear to have so much as a single sexual thought, let a single desire so much as flicker in my mind, during the two years after I was widowed. Not only because my grief made me loyal to my wife, but also because I was grieving for someone who was dead, and death is such a physical thing. I didn't want physical things. I didn't even like facts about things, and in a secret way I came to hate the truth itself.

This extra dimension of loneliness, this revulsion for the world and even, at first, for the stuff of which it was composed, seemed unique at the time. But I think I see now that it was completely typical, and that what revolted me above all was the understanding that everything passes away.

So this sad insight didn't first visit me while I waited with Flower for something to happen between us. And she wasn't the woman who broke me out of the ice. A month or so after the second anniversary of my widowhood, I went to a prostitute. Or rather, she came to me, came to my hotel room in Washington where I was staying at the expense of the Senate Committee on Ethics, who were conducting hearings. (I was called to Washington, but never called to testify.) A tall woman in her thirties, the only prostitute I've ever met as such. I explained my situation to her, and she was very understanding, and she even refused payment, and we made love. At first she refused payment, that is, but afterward she suddenly wondered if I hadn't been conning her with a sad story, and she wanted her money on general principles. Ultimately she decided I couldn't have been so false about a part of life so real, and wouldn't take the money. But I insisted. So she took it. And that is how that went.

I didn't feel villainous, or soiled, either. I felt like I'd been with a woman, we'd meant something to each other, maybe not very much, and she'd passed along.

So this isn't about that at all.

Am I making sense in this account? Am I intelligible? Or am I muttering? I think it stands a chance of being useful. That's the point of writing it all down. It's not just an aid to private introspection. But am I being too meditative? Too introspective?

The joint of Flower's collarbones showed in the neck of her smock, and just below it the moles and imperfections in the flesh on her breastbone. To let my wife and child be dead. I didn't think I was cruel enough for that. Because that is what the imperfections in Flower's skin invited me to do. There was a sense in which Anne and Elsie had to be killed, and killing them was up to me.

I had to break the tension, the mixed desire and shame, I had to say anything at all. "I'd like to read the phrases inside your envelopes. Let me see what other people wrote."

"I can't let you do that."

"Why not?"

"Because then when these words are all closed up inside this box they won't be in a dark place anymore. Light will leak in and they'll slowly get eaten up. A dim light. A deteriorating light. The light that comes from your mind."

"What do you mean? My mind in particular, or anybody who happens to read them?"

"Anybody's mind. If anybody finds out what they say, their perfection will slowly deteriorate."

"But you know, don't you? You've read them."

"Yes. But if anybody else ever does, then what they're doing inside me will be destroyed."

She looked at me now with a very vivid, communicative expression on her lovely face. It said she was quite willing to view all this as absurd and humorous, but her eyes emanated a deep curiosity to see if I might somehow understand. I think I did understand. But I don't think she believed I did.

And I did kiss her. Touched her sleeve with my fingers. She didn't draw away. I plucked at her sleeve and she came close and I put my lips to hers.

"Okay," she said. "Come back inside, please."

She took me by the hand, carrying her box in the crook of her arm. On the way in she toed the rubber-tipped stopper with her pointed boot, and the heavy door swung to behind us. She set the box of phrases beside her pallet in the classroom and we descended onto the folds of nylon—it was a sleeping bag, not much of a cushion against the concrete floor. For a few minutes we kissed wildly, but I felt like a man in the wrong neighborhood, expecting at any moment to turn onto the right street, wondering where the hell it is and growing more and more panicked and disoriented. She was sweet, nothing about her felt held back, no slight deflection, no place reserved for herself, no irony or mischief, no studious objectivity, none of the stratagems that might have kept part of her out of this dalliance with an old man.

"Tell me your dream. The one you wouldn't tell me."

"I saw you in a room full of strangers. On a stage. They were studying you. It was just a dream."

Kissing me, she unbuckled my belt and I helped with the rest. In my white boxer shorts I gave back her kisses and we both worked at the top buttons of her smock.

"This isn't it," I said. I felt no desire for her now. With a distinct and physical sensation I was slipping back into that hole where I felt no desire at all. I gripped her hands tight but it didn't help. "I'm leaving." I clutched at my clothing, snatched up whatever looked like mine from the floor and covered myself.

"I'm so sorry," I said.

My shirt open, barefoot, I got out to my car and tossed my shoes and socks into the back seat and hung on desperately to the steering wheel. She stood on the steps, just a shape. A shape containing . . .

This—now—was the point I'd wanted to reach with her. All the expected moments had been stepped through. One step more would take us into moments that could never have been foretold. I opened the door and put my feet out and pulled on my shoes. I buttoned my shirt, I watched her shape. I turned off the motor and went back.

She wasn't there. The shape of her may not have been there in the first place. I went up the front steps and down the steps inside.

She stood still at the end of the hallway, having hesitated, I guessed, at the sound of my footfalls coming. She'd opened the back door again. From outside a warm green breath filled the hallway and began moving through it softly and audibly.

She came toward me carrying her message from a vanished god. "Would you like to hear the story of my name?"

I had a sense of her studio, just to my right, filled with ghostly items and skeletal things.

Again: "Would you like me to tell you the story of my name?"

I followed her back into her studio and sat on the spangled chair.

"First I think I have to tell you another story before I can tell you the story of my name."

I didn't say a word.

"An illustrated tale. Not just a story—a picture, too."

Looking for something or other, she wandered among her objects, these multifarious seashells, sprays of baby's breath, sprays of peacock feathers like abstract eyes on white necks, many-colored balls of yarn, tinfoil collected into shiny knots, miniature bottles you could fill to overflowing from a thimble, somber and translucent, purple, blue, green. She'd made her world a space for these things, for the train cars and props of model railroads, particularly the engines, small and black and heavy engines; birds' nests cradling eggshells of turquoise and mottled amber: things whose perishing had been arrested by their power to make her love them. Objects not stored in boxes and labeled for eventual use, but left out in plain sight to be found and contemplated. Left open to encounters with strangers.

"Before I can tell you the story of my name," Flower said, "I believe I have to tell you the story of your face."

I felt better when she said that. "A sad, ugly tale."

"I don't want to! But it's necessary."

She'd found a sketch pad, a sheaf of newsprint in large sheets. She sat on a stool behind the nearest easel, set up the pad, took a thick pencil from the easel's tray, and began, I guessed, to draw. She was left-handed.

"Your lips are thin. You have a big space between your nose and upper lip, like a monkey, but you miss having a monkey face because your chin is too small and there's not enough face beneath your mouth to make a monkey face. Your nose is small and pushed up too far. Too much of your nostrils show. That makes your eyes look sort of dull-minded and also sort of fearful."

She stopped momentarily and honed her pencil on a piece of emery paper.

"Your eyes are a very beautiful blue. You have nice round cheeks, and bushy well-defined eyebrows. Very definite eyebrows. Your hair is nice, very tightly curled, kinked, really, and with lots of colors in it, brown and blond and some blue and mostly gray. And you're small."

Flower stood up and held the sketch pad out before her at arm's length a full minute, looking back and forth between her rendering and her model. She turned the pad to me. It was quick, but recognizable.

"Your hands are small. I've told you you have an inner and outer smallness that's very attractive, at least to me."

"Thank you. I think."

"The story of your face is over."

"Thank you even more."

"Now the other story. Once I was taken away by a guy to a gingerbread house."

"Excuse me?"

"This is the story of my name."

"Okay. All right."

"When I was a little girl, one day a man led me away from my home and took me to a gingerbread house.

"He was small like you, Michael, and his nose was turned up too far, like yours, and his chin was too small like yours. But his face was narrow, and his whole head, too, and his ears were big and funny. Not like yours. You have nice ears.

"I was four years old. One morning he came to our back yard and took me away. They didn't find me till after dark.

"He sang a song," she said.

"Were you terrified?"

"I wasn't. And I'm not terrified when I remember. But everyone I've ever told it to has been."

(She looked at me quizzically, searching, I suppose, for m
fear. I'm sure it was there and I'm sure she discovered it.

(Yet now these words came from me—I didn't intend them
and I didn't even know what they meant—I just remember
them now—I hear them—I said, "I still can't feel anything."
No response from Flower. Maybe she didn't hear.)

"I don't remember much. Sometimes when I'm trying to
recall what happened, I think I remember another little girl
there. An almost sad little girl watching me. I didn't think of
sadness then, so I don't know, but I almost think she was sad.
Here's what else I remember:

"In the morning I was playing in the garden. I had some
mischief in my mind. The back yard was bordered all around
by a flower bed about six feet wide, all along the base of this
cinderblock wall that enclosed the yard. It was the spring season. I looked in the earth where I sort of understood, without
actually remembering doing it, that my mother and sisters and
I had planted bulbs in the fall, tulip bulbs, and I sensed there
were tulips growing there right now, just under the dirt. I
wanted to dig there and see. It was a mischief in my mind. I
didn't care if I disturbed the tulips.

"I saw the man standing in the corner of the yard. He'd
walked in the flower bed, I could see his footprints as clearly as
the footprints in a cartoon or a comic book, big, funny
shoeprints with nothing else around them. I'm supposing he
was a small man. I know how he looked to me—I can close
my eyes and look right now. He seems just the right size, a
friendly size, not an intimidating size like most grown-ups.

. is very narrow, very sort of wedgelike. He's look-
ie's been watching me as I study the bare flower
e says,

were a girl I'd want to be a flower.'

quick I tell him, 'I'm a flower!'

e you a flower?'

lidn't know what to say. I'd wanted him to tell me, 'Yes!
a flower!' but he didn't quite do that, did he?

I can't see very much else about him, nothing that I'm
is real. I think he's wearing brown corduroy pants and a
yed sweater, but I maybe imagined them later, added them
a my own later on.

"He said, 'I can put you on the wall. Can I put you on the
wall? I won't let you tumble.'

"My mom's in the kitchen maybe twenty feet away. She's
got her stereo cranked up playing music, loud music—"

(I interrupted: "What music?" I asked. "Hippie-type rock
'n' roll," she said. I realized it had to be so—but I imagined the
hymn of the Frieslanders playing.)

"When he had me sitting on the wall he told me, 'I can
climb.'

"He climbed onto the wall. 'Watch me climb.'

"And he came down on the other side, saying, 'Can I take
you down from the wall? Let me.'

"He showed me a car parked there in the dirt lane between
the houses. He said, 'Here's my car.' I don't remember what it
looked like.

"I don't remember being in his car, or moving or traveling. I remember a forest all around, like a story I'd always known about, like meeting a celebrity everyone knows about. The famous forest. The forest from fairy tales and bedtime stories.

"I remember the inside of a very small room with a very low ceiling and I remember knowing that this was his home, where I sat in a small chair and he sat in a big one, and that it was a gingerbread home. Whenever I've smelled ginger since then, these memories come back so strong and so fast I get dizzy.

"I don't have much of my time there. I know we talked, or he said things to me that I didn't find very important. I was waiting for something else, for someone to come, for an event or a show to start—that was the feeling I had: I was waiting. This part didn't count, sitting here, because I was waiting for something else.

"I think we sat there for a long time. Maybe hours. I was gone many hours, I do know that, and I don't remember doing anything but sitting in that very small room like the inside of a mushroom, and I remember thinking, This is a gingerbread house, and this room is a mushroom. I thought this was a fictional man who turned out to be real, just as the forest of fiction had turned real.

"We sat in the mushroom in the gingerbread house. It was dim and small in there. He talked, and I don't remember. I remember only two things:

"He said to me, 'She's blind.'

" 'Who is blind?'

"But he didn't answer. I thought he didn't know the answer. That he knew someone was blind, but that he didn't know who.

"He sang a song. I don't know the song.

"If I ever hear it in my life again I'm sure I'll recognize it. But I can't call up any memory of the song, or really any image of him singing. I just remember knowing that the man in the gingerbread house sang a song. And I remember that he said to me, 'She's blind,' and I said, 'Who is blind?' and he didn't answer."

(As for me, the listener, you'd think sitting still would have given me some control. Instead I was getting more and more worked up. The feeling that I'd been released from God's power left me removed, but removed to a realm of emotion, a cauldron. I saw Flower presenting her nakedness on a glaring stage, small and perfect and surrounded by darkness, like a scene in a secret grotto.)

"All morning the whole neighborhood searched for me. By afternoon the police were involved. Well after dark, two cops found me by the road at the edge of the woods. I hadn't really been afraid of the little man at all. But the two cops scared me so much I couldn't stop bawling. They tried to be nice, but they were like giant robots. Their car was like a horrible spaceship.

"They asked me where I'd been, but I didn't answer. Later I thought about it, remembered what there was to remember. I've remembered ever since.

"I remember he said, 'She's blind. And her name is Flower.'

" 'Is it me?' I asked him. 'Is that my name?'

"That's when I remember the other little girl. I don't see her. I just kind of remember I knew she was there. That he said her name was Flower.

"And so my name became Flower, too."

Flower sat beside her easel and watched me long enough in silence that I understood her story was finished.

I asked her, "What's your name—your real name?"

"My name is really and legally Flower Cannon."

"But not originally? Originally what was your name?"

"Micah. Micah James. No Middle Name."

"That's just as beautiful . . . But James?"

"My mother's name was James. They didn't get married till I was seven, just after Kali was born. I don't think they planned on getting married right then, or they wouldn't have named her Kali—not when her last name would be Cannon. 'Kali Cannon!' At that time I changed my name legally to Flower. Or rather my parents had it changed, because I asked them to.

"I didn't talk about what happened. I didn't tell my parents for years. When I did tell them, it made them momentarily crazy, my mom anyway. My mom stood up in her living room and lifted the coffee table over her head and broke it over the back of a chair. They'd never asked, and that's the reason I'd never told them.

"At first I sort of assumed they knew, as if they could have seen, as if my life were on TV and they were of course watching my show, the show that was the story of my name.

"Otherwise I've told very few people. And never any man except my father, until now, until you. It's not a secret, but it's very valuable and I haven't really felt like taking it out and showing it to anybody for fear they might come back later somehow, and somehow they might steal it. Steal it and put another one in its place that looks and feels right but isn't the real story, isn't really as valuable."

"Flower. Why tell me?" It was a desperate question.

"Why? Because you have the right face for this. You understand what this man looks like. The man in the story. Because in certain important ways you look like him. No, you don't look alike, but I think he had the same feeling when he looked at himself in the mirror. The same feeling you get when you look at your face. *If* you look. Do you look, Michael?"

"No."

"No. You wash it, you shave it, you don't look. But you used to look?"

"A long time ago. In my teens, I guess."

"Later I remembered the little girl. I'm sure she was watching me. She wasn't blind."

—This was what flooded the basement with fear, this simple statement: "I'm sure she was watching me. She wasn't blind." What connected these words from Flower's lips to the accident that killed my family? From them I understood that I could no longer bear my daughter's death. It was going to break me. And I would have to let it.

I'm not sure I said goodbye. The tide of my own confusion carried me out of the room and up out of the building. Once

again I was in my car, and this time I was going. The old
building hunched there in a dusk that seemed to get paler
rather than darker as the light leached out of it. I could make
out the shape of Flower's face at the basement window, watching, I suppose. Was her story the story of a ghost? The ghost of
my daughter? I started the car and pulled away.

I haven't seen or heard of her since.

I got it into gear and onto the Old Highway and drove
east, running away from the sunlit rim of the plains. I wasn't
traveling fast, not at first, but the rows of cultivation whipped
quickly by, and in the dizzying exactness of their changing
perspective they turned and opened and closed again as I shot
down the middle of the fields. I accelerated but I still felt as if
I had stepped wrong and was plunging backward. Like the
rider on an amusement, I had that strange satisfaction that it
was all designed to be scary, to be fun, and would soon be
over. I wondered if that meant I was going to die. I had no
reason to think I would, but I wondered. I put my foot to the
floor and stared straight forward while the terror of high
speed opened up the sinuses in my head and put a taste of
pennies in my mouth. And I drove like a spear through the
tiny towns, miniatures in a work of meticulous depiction
floating on the fields of corn and soy, went speeding along
through them toward some deep violent conclusion—to have
my heart torn out and eaten while I watched. The sun had set
but the fields were soaked with light in the dusk. I wanted to
stagger to the shore of this mindless iridescence and throw
into it my most beloved thing, my very favorite thing. When

I'd worn myself out going too fast, I pulled into the roadside weeds. I stopped the car in the middle of the round shimmering table of the earth. Meanwhile the dusk wouldn't die. Everything was visible and there was even enough light to read the title of the pamphlet from the Friesland Fellowship: "Come to the Father."

I picked it up from the dashboard and read its few paragraphs. I found myself disappointed by what it said. Its author stressed that an inward experience of conversion was important. In my current frame of mind I'd hoped for warnings much stranger and not so obvious: "Brown shoes are important." "Attention to the length of the fingernails is crucial." "Everything depends on the sky."

On the very brink of making love to her, I hadn't seen Flower naked. More than once I'd seen her stripped completely bare, but not this time. She'd had her smock unbuttoned, that was all. This time I'd been the one stripped bare. A nakedness both sudden and long in coming. Did she do that to me? Or did it simply coincide?

I thought of what she'd said, in my mind I heard her saying it, I couldn't stop hearing it, I wished she'd never said it:

"I'm sure she was watching me. She wasn't blind."

I drove on toward the world's darker half. Now the horizon was like that of the sea around certain islands, tar black, blended with the night. Halfway up the sky and to my right floated the new moon. Satisfied that darkness had found me, feeling in a way hidden from myself, I put the car in gear and went to my home.

—Which I reached within an hour. I spent a good long while opening the door, which I'd never operated, of my house's small garage, and parked the BMW. In the dimness I couldn't make out the color of this vehicle, and I hadn't bothered to notice in the light. I can't think of any more significant betrayal in my life, that is, any clearer contradicton of a former self, than owning this car after four years' mourning two victims of a car crash. I pressed the button and stepped out quickly as the door rolled shut. I stood on the walk looking up at a hazy sky from which nevertheless a bit of starlight descended. The waterfall noise of a stadium crowd reached me, exploding and fading. A block away we had the high school, the town's biggest, or so I understood: low penitentiary structures and trampled grounds. In the mornings, clumps of students plied the neighborhood. I wasn't around to see what they got up to in the afternoons.

I took a liter bottle of Pellegrino from my refrigerator and walked over to the high school, where a night baseball game was in progress. The stadium lay in a vale—a dell?—one of the few significant depressions in the area's landscape. The whole world had seeped away and down into this bowl. The playing field below me was utterly green with vegetable life and white with electric light, floating in an empty blackness.

I watched the rest of the game. It seemed an important one. The fans behaved like an excited, roaring liquid. Over this distance I couldn't make out the ball itself, had no evidence of it except the occasional very small tick of it against a bat, so all this complicated behavior, all the grace of the players and the commotion in response, seemed to be about nothing.

I thought of Flower Cannon, of her studio like a sunken cave, her tiny incidental treasures, her collection of envelopes. I wished I could see the phrases the others had written. I was sure she'd led each of us to a moment when a drop of essence sprang out—something delicately insane, not at all "tame"— and then captured it in her box of handwriting. I was sure her cedar box was a beautiful zoo of wild utterances. And the finest accomplishment of her art.

I couldn't turn it off, the memory of her voice: "She was watching me. She wasn't blind."

I remained looking down on the ballfield until the sound of departing cars died almost completely, until the bleachers lay skeletal and deserted, until suddenly the floodlights went off with a *thunk*, producing a darkness that momentarily felt not only deep but entirely personal to me. My eyes came back and the simple night returned around me and I got up and walked off dusting my seat, shifting my nearly empty bottle of Pellegrino from hand to hand. When a car full of boys sailed past whooping—whooping at me, it seemed—I shouted, "Quiet!" and they yelled, "Fuck you!" in reply. "Fuck *you*!" I yelled back. They turned the car around at the corner and went past me again, all the occupants squawking unintelligibly like the wheels on a passing train.

"FUCK YOU!" I screamed.

The car slammed to a halt. Its tires thumped over the right-hand curb and then the left as it made a quick wide U-turn and roared back toward me in the lowest, loudest gear. The oncoming glare struck my head like lightning in a bare room.

I flung my bottle with everything I had, right from the earth up. I put so much into the effort that it yanked at the tendons in my legs, behind my knees. Even above the engine's commotion I heard a sharp clunk, and fracturing glass.

The car jigged sideways just before crushing me, hopped onto the grassy margin, slid across it, and stopped some twenty yards away. A black star, full of an atomic potential, dark and fraught. It rumbled and breathed. For several seconds, nothing else. Then it suddenly burst apart, all four doors, and divided into its constituents like an egg-sack.

They came at me, several boys, I couldn't guess how many, and in the face of their headlong strength and life I felt myself filling like a balloon; filled to bursting; filled with spitting rage. How I'd longed for this as a teacher!—to charge at a squad of students, to grapple with as many as I could get my hands on and go down in the dirt clawing, kicking, biting. I gouged at their eyes and mouths, took an elbow in the eye, a knee to the kidneys. I wanted to get at least one of them by the throat.

"What's wrong with this guy!"

"What is wrong with you!"

"He's crazy! He's out of his mind!"

"You're insane! You're manic-depressive or something!"

"YOU CRAZY BASTARD."

In no time they had me pinned against the car, a couple of grunting boys on each outflung arm while another, on his belly, embraced my ankles.

"FIVE AGAINST ONE!" I hollered.

"This is gonna cost you! This is definitely gonna cost you! And you better pay! That's my dad's car!"

"I'll fight you one at a time," I said. And I'm afraid I *was* crazy, and I meant it. I started the struggle again when hands frisked my pockets.

"Look! Hold still! Just—I'm not robbing you! I just want your license!"

One boy had let go of me—the one whose dad owned the car—and taken hold of his own head with both his hands. He marched back and forth. "We could say it was a small accident! Like when you, when you, when you—I don't know!" He let go of his head. "Do you have insurance? You *better* have insurance. We'll just take your name, your number on the license—where's his license?"

"He doesn't have a wallet. Don't you have a wallet?"

"It's at home."

"You threw a *rock* at my *car*!" the driver said. "How *old* are you?"

A good question. I was starting to feel miserable now. Just the same I thought I might yet punch this kid in the face. "I'm only about a block over, guys," I said. "Come on and I'll give you some ID." It struck me that I'd been driving for two days without a valid license. Mine was years expired, issued half a continent away.

"I'm not letting you in my dad's car!"

"And I wouldn't get in anyhow," I said. "I'm walking."

"Don't think you're getting away! I'm right on your ass!

I don't care if you—I don't care if you—" He couldn't say what.

They followed me in the car, driving very slowly and discussing me audibly. They seemed to be coming to the solid conclusion amongst themselves that I was schizophrenic.

"Do you *live* here?" the driver said when he saw the inside of my house.

"You have this persistent tone of alarm," I told him. "Will you cut it out?"

"It's bare! You're all boxed up! When are you leaving?"

"I'm not going anywhere. I don't even own a car"—a precise but misleading fact I felt happy to divulge. The truth was I'd started to share his suspicion I might just flee in the night.

I had, I think, nine boxes and a suitcase, and a plan, or a hope, for getting them all in the car. I would have shipped the majority of them but they had no destination.

"God! You're worse than a kid!" the boy said.

All five of them stood on my small porch, shouldering each other aside to peek through the open door into the dark interior while I found my wallet in my linen sports jacket.

The driver consulted with the others until he grasped that consulting with them couldn't help, they were all so young and drunk and perplexed and entertained by his trouble, and then he decided he had to call the police.

I let them all inside while he used the phone. In my living room now wallowed a sort of monster of callow health and well-being.

"Nothing but boxes," one repeated.

"Can't you turn on a light?"

"Listen, you punk," I said. "The numbers *light up* when you pick up the phone. Otherwise you can go downtown and use a pay phone." I might say anything now. By the minute I felt more and more out of bounds and ridiculous, more and more stupid and mad at myself.

Two policemen arrived in a squad car to find us all standing out front in an arrangement like that of a field sport: five teammates surrounding a guy who might break into a run. One officer took charge while the second stood quietly beside him and arbitrated by saying "Sh!" now and then to the youngsters.

The boy explained the situation quickly but repeatedly, using many times the phrases "My father's car!" and "We were just driving along!"

"This license the most recent one you have?" the officer asked me. I told him yes.

"His house is full of boxes! He's *moving*, Officer. My father's car!"

"How much have you had to drink tonight, son?"

"Me?"

"You're the one I'm talking to."

"Me? Okay. A couple—"

A second spoke up. "I didn't have any, Officer. And I'm the one driving."

"Okay," another friend said. "We had two six-packs. That's—two beers each, right?"

"We just want to be honest, Officer."

"We were headed straight home. We were headed straight home."

"You boys go to Henry Harris?"

"Yessir. We were at the game. We were headed safely home."

"Honest, Officer, I didn't have one beer, I swear to God."

"Then you be the one to drive your friends home." The officer shone his flashlight now into every face, mine too, and took a quick emphatic decision. "In terms of what's happening now: I'm not gonna try and cope with you all and your silliness tonight. We'll take this up at the station in the morning when everybody's sober."

"His house is full of *boxes*—he's leaving town!"

"I'm getting all the information off his driver's license and faculty ID."

"*Faculty!* He's on the *faculty*? What kind of faculty did they allow *him* on? You should be fired," the boy concluded.

"Otherwise I put you on a blow-machine, son, and we get you for Minor in Possession."

"Oh," the boy said. "I'm sorry. I didn't understand. Thank you, Officer."

The others said thank-you with a murmuring humility all the more pitiful for being genuine.

The Officer said, "Mr. Reed. You'll be there tomorrow, right?"

"Just say when." But I didn't intend to deal with this. I felt happy and alive and I would leave town that night, in my BMW full of boxes, driving fast, well over the limit.

"If my dad doesn't get the money for that windshield—"

"Son. He'll be there. And you, too, you'll be there. Everybody sober, eight A.M."

"Eight!"

"Hey. I usually go home at seven. I'll be staying overtime just for you."

"Us too? All of us?" another said.

"One of you better come along. Whoever of you, I don't care. Just so we have two witnesses."

The boy whose father owned the damaged vehicle took hold of my hand and shook it with a kind of post-cathartic goodwill. "I'll see you in the morning, Sir. Don't worry," he told us all, his friends, myself, the cop, the sky of stars, "I think he's just a schizophrenic. We'll work this out."

I left town before dawn. I never heard anything more about any of this. Apparently, crimes on a petty level can actually be waltzed away from.

I didn't drive straight out of town. I made a brief side trip to visit the mystery, I guess I'll say, of a pair of personal symbols: the monolith and the circular skating rink—now, in summer, a flat pool reflecting the midnight sky. My car sat a hundred yards off in a loading zone behind the student-union building with a front door open and the interior illuminated dimly. I stood at the rail looking down at the black of space and the silver clouds floating past my feet. Summer classes hadn't started, at two A.M. there wasn't a soul around, certainly nobody skating. And I missed them, and I missed the curiosity and estrangement and hope with which I'd breathed the winter air in the movie I'd inhabited briefly before it had ended. I missed the hunger.

As I write this, a Mediterranean breeze comes in through the open window. I'm writing half naked, in white socks and white boxer shorts purchased in Athens. A stack of books holds down my typesheets; on top of the books rests a chunk of the Berlin Wall, or so I'm happy to believe. I won it last October from a journalist during an afternoon of gin rummy, also of gin and vermouth. These days, and for some time now, I myself am a journalist.

I stopped here off the Greek coast to write a lengthy piece, a historical sketch of the Slavic troubles. The books, the maps, my notes just sit there. From the first day I've done nothing but remember the past. The small breeze here tastes as if it comes across miles of early summer corn. The sky has that relentless emptiness the sky can have on a hot day over the endless farms. This island is a big arid solitary rock that pleads for a sculptor to come. To the south and west it has no neighbors. And my window faces that direction. On any calm day when the seas are low the horizon looks like that of the tamed and subjugated Midwestern prairies with which for a time I allowed myself to be surrounded.

I left the Midwest without goodbyes. For about three months, the rest of that summer and into the fall, I stayed in a converted boat-house in Hyder, Alaska, the state's southernmost region, a strip of coast that runs alongside British Columbia. I spent the long days reading books and listening to recorded music. I really did almost nothing else. One night about ten, when the colossal red presence of the sunset was crashing into the big studio and I was just bending over the tub and putting the plug in the drain to draw myself a bath, a drop of liquid struck my wrist, and then another. I glanced up to see if some pipe overhead were leaking, and then I felt it: tears running down my cheeks. I slipped to my knees, my head hanging, face lolling into the tub, and rested in that position while I sobbed out loud, bawled and shook like a child all through the hour of sundown until it was dark . . . When I pulled the light-chain I saw that I'd wept so profusely and for so long that a tiny flood of my own tears, enough to fill a shot glass, had pooled in the drain. I was about to pull the plug when I thought better of it. I turned on the faucet and filled the tub and stripped naked and soaked, exhausted by grief and joy, until my bath was cold.

The next winter I took an assignment to cover the Gulf War. I arrived in Dahran, Saudi Arabia, six days before the U.N. bombing campaign began. Soon Scud missiles began blowing up over the city.

I've taken assignments steadily since then. I remain a student of history, more of one than ever, now that our century has torn its way out of its chrysalis and become too beautiful to be examined, too alive to be debated and exploited by played-out intellectuals. The important thing is no longer to predict in what way its grand convulsions might next shake us. Now the important thing is to ride it into the sky.

After three weeks in Dahran I moved to the north, the town of Nuaryriyah. Off and on, for a while, I traveled around the uniform emptiness of the Hijarah Desert interviewing American soldiers at the gates of their encampments. I spent many nights near the Iraqi border sleeping inside my rented Toyota in the middle of a vast waste. The desert trembled with incessant bombing, rumbled so deeply it couldn't actually be heard. I was there, I felt it, it thudded in the soul. I wore khakis and desert boots and an Australian commando's hat. My face burned brown in the sun. I was adopted by a group of junior executives (what else to call them?—they were young engineers, computer jocks, even an accountant, from Parker-Boyd, a civilian helicopter-maintenance firm under contract to the military in the Gulf) who erroneously understood me to have permission to travel anywhere in the region. With them and their crews and guards of bulky, invulnerable-looking young Marines I flew in helicopters above blazing tank battles in the desert in the night, through black smoke overclouding a world pocked by burning oil wells like flickering signals of distress, of helplessness, floated like prey in the talons of a hawk above a bare brown planet with nothing in it but two or three roads and a war; and continued day after day in a life I believe to be utterly remarkable.

About the Author

Denis Johnson is the author of *Already Dead, Jesus' Son, Resuscitation of a Hanged Man, Fiskadoro, The Stars at Noon,* and *Angels.* His poetry has been collected in the volume *The Throne of the Third Heaven of the Nations Millennium General Assembly.* He is the recipient of a Lannan Fellowship and a Whiting Writer's Award, among many other awards for his work. He lives in northern Idaho.

GEORGE -
718 - 857 - 1885
212 - 620 - 7119
DAVIDSON.GEORGE@DOL.GOV

212 - 365 - 0936

516 - 0624

9698

917-715-

14388 5752 2078 5457

15.

557

905

s/w

- 212 - 255 - 9655
X 16 (0)

WEBMASTER

info@breadmyl.roooo.com

1326

988